James Payn

Walter's Word

Vol. III

James Payn

Walter's Word
Vol. III

ISBN/EAN: 9783337047511

Printed in Europe, USA, Canada, Australia, Japan

Cover: Foto ©Andreas Hilbeck / pixelio.de

More available books at **www.hansebooks.com**

WALTER'S WORD.

A Novel.

BY

JAMES PAYN,

AUTHOR OF "LOST SIR MASSINGBERD," "AT HER MERCY," ETC. ETC.

IN THREE VOLUMES.

VOL. III.

LONDON:

TINSLEY BROTHERS, 8, CATHERINE STREET, STRAND.

1875.

CONTENTS

OF

THE THIRD VOLUME.

WALTER'S WORD.

CHAPTER I.

FIXING THE PRICE.

ON hearing the answering cry from their comrades the party pushed up the hill, and presently came upon a level lawn, surrounded with fine trees, each a leafy tent, since their branches descended to the ground, so as to form shelter from rain or sun; a brook babbled down its centre, and by its side were tethered sheep and goats. Nor did this pastoral scene lack more romantic elements, for beside the sheep, instead of shepherds, lay, wooing the morning sun, the main body of the brigand band, some thirty men, scarcely any of whom had yet reached middle life, and bedizened in such finery as only children or savages could elsewhere have found a pleasure in wearing. The pistols stuck in their gay scarves, and the muskets piled in the centre of the lawn, suggested a company of amateur actors rehearsing some exquisite *tableau vivant*, after Salvator Rosa, rather than what they really were—a band of bloodshedders and ruffians. They jumped up with a shout of welcome as the newcomers made their appearance, and crowded around Walter with signs of great excitement and a continuous chatter, of which he could make nothing, but which was probably concerning his market value in ducats. Then some one cried out, " Il Capitano," and these inquisitive gentry melted away from him as if by magic, and Corralli himself stood before him with outstretched hand.

" Welcome, signor, to our country-house," said he, smiling. " I cannot say that I hope to see you long here; but while you are with us, you shall have no cause to complain of our hospitality."

Walter's mind and eyes were wandering from tree to tree, in speculation as to which might form the bower of Lilian; but he made shift to make some civil response to this greeting—the courtesy of which he set down at its just value. It was evident that the brigand chief required something of him beside his ransom.

"Your friends in Palermo——"

"I have no friends there," interrupted Walter quickly.

"Well, well; those, then, who miscall themselves your friends, have been very injudicious: but for their having sent out the troops, Milord and his daughter might by this time have been on board their yacht again. As it is, there is no knowing when they may be—if ever." And at these last two words, which were uttered very sternly, that ugly look came over the brigand's face which seemed to reveal the character of the man behind it.

"Where is Milord, as you persist so wrongfully in calling him?"

"You shall see him in a few moments. I have sent for you here indeed for that purpose. Look, sir; what you have told me of yourself and your slender purse may be true or not." Walter was about to speak, but the other stopped him with a gesture. "Let us suppose it true, then; it is my rule that cannot is the same as will not; and when the ransom is not forthcoming, I kill the captive. Your life is therefore forfeit. I might say much more than your life, but I do not wish to proceed to extremities with you, even in the way of menace. You may save your skin without the loss of a ducat if you will only be guided by good sense."

Walter bowed his head. "What is it you require of me, Captain Corralli?"

"I want you to teach reason to this fellow-countryman of yours, whom I have in my power."

"And his daughter, where is his daughter?"

"She is safe enough. No harm will happen to her, from us at all events."

"That means that she is dying," answered Walter hoarsely. "If the damp and cold should kill her, you are none the less her murderer than if you had slain her with your hands."

"I will settle with my own conscience for that, signor," returned the other contemptuously. "What we are both concerned about at present—and you much more than I, believe me—is this ransom. The old man is a fool, and can be made to understand nothing. He does not comprehend that I shall burn him alive, skin him alive; he thinks he is in London, and has to deal with a mere pickpocket. I protest that he offered me one thousand ducats—not a week's living for the band. It made my fingers itch to shoot him down, only that that would have been letting him off too cheaply."

So furious was the brigand's passion that the foam flew from his lips, his eyes glared like those of a wild beast, and his fingers roved from knife-handle to pistol-butt as though they had been the keys of a piano.

"What is it exactly you wish me to do?" inquired Walter.

"To convince him that I mean what I say, that what I threaten I will perform; and worse, that if this money I demand is not forthcoming—all of it—that he shall die, and be days in dying; that he shall pray for death a thousand times, and in vain."

"And what am I to gain if I am successful in persuading him, Captain Corralli?"

"Life, liberty! His ransom shall cover yours, which is but a flea-bite. If you fail, beware young man, for you shall share his fate. Now follow me." With these words, delivered in a most menacing tone, Corralli turned upon his heel, and led the way to a large beech-tree, the branches of which swept the ground, and moving them aside revealed to Walter's eyes the recumbent form of Mr. Christopher Brown, wrapped in a capote, and pillowed on one of the cushions stolen from the cabin of his yacht.

The old merchant had not been sleeping; anxiety and discomfort had banished slumber from him; but as he rose upon his elbow to regard his visitors, he rubbed his eyes, like some newly-awakened man, who doubts whether he is not still in the land of dreams.

"Why, that's not Mr. Litton, surely?"

His tone had no displeasure in it, such as Walter had apprehended; the danger and strangeness of his position forbade his entertaining the ideas which might naturally have occurred to him under ordinary circumstances; he did not recognise in Walter

the man whom he had dismissed from
his own house for deceit, whom he suspected of plotting to win his daughter, and
whose very presence in Sicily at the present
moment he might well associate with the
pursuit of the same forbidden object; he
only beheld a friend and fellow-countryman,
dropped out of the clouds, and, as he
vaguely hoped, with power to succour
him.

"Why, who would have thought of meeting you in this den of thieves!" continued
Mr. Brown. "Do you bring any good
news?"

"Indeed, sir, no," answered Walter sorrow-
fully; "I am only this man's prisoner, like
yourself."

"Yes, yes; all mice in my trap," put in
Corralli, understanding by Walter's manner
what was meant, and gesticulating triumphantly with his fingers. "Two were caught
first, click, click! and then this one came to
look after them, click!"

"What does the wretch say?" inquired
Mr. Brown.

"He is telling you how it happens that
I am here. I had discovered you were

captured, and on my road to give the alarm
I got taken prisoner myself."

"I am sorry that we have done you such
a wrong," said the merchant with feeling.

"I shall not regret it, Mr. Brown, if only
I may be the means of being of advantage
to you," answered Walter. "At present
our position is very serious. The troops
have been called out, which has enraged the
brigands, and——"

"But surely then we are certain of
rescue?" interrupted the merchant eagerly.
"The soldiers must needs make short work
of such scoundrels as these."

"If they could only catch them; but that
is not so easy. And if they did so, they
would not find us alive. It is this man's
invariable custom to kill his captives, if he
cannot keep them."

"That is what he has been trying to persuade me all along," said Mr. Brown; "but
I am not going to believe such nonsense.
We are British subjects, and the thing is
incredible, Mr. Litton. I would have dared
him to do his worst, had it not been for dear
Lilian." Here the old man's lips began to
quiver, and a tear stole down his white

cheek. "She was weak and ailing when they took her, and though I have reason to believe she is better lodged than I have been, and attended by persons of her own sex, I tremble for what may be the effects of such rude treatment. Oh, Mr. Litton, what an ass and idiot I was to listen to Sir Reginald's advice, and leave old England for such a country as this! How long do you think it will be before we get out of it?"

"It is impossible, my dear sir, to guess at that. What I would implore you to persuade yourself is, that your position is a matter of life and death, in which no sacrifice can be considered too great. I am instructed by this man to treat with you concerning your ransom."

"Yes, yes," cried Corralli, pricking up his ears at the familiar 'word;' "now you are coming to it at last. It is well you should make Milord come to reason."

"What I would advise, Mr. Brown," said Walter, "is that you should be firm on one point—namely, to pay nothing whatever until your daughter is placed in safety with her sister."

"How much does he say?" exclaimed

Corralli impatiently. " I should like to hear him come to the point. Will he pay me my six hundred thousand ducats ?"

" You must be mad, Captain Corralli," exclaimed Walter in amazement. "There is no man alive, unless you caught your king himself, who could pay such a sum as that."

" You mean no Sicilian ; but there are plenty Inglese. They are made of gold ; I know it. Nothing is good enough for them, and nothing too dear. A man who has a pleasure ship of his own too ! My demands are too moderate ; if anything is amiss with them, that is it. You tell him what I say. Six hundred thousand ducats, or he is a dead man."

" This man says, Mr. Brown, that you must pay him a hundred thousand pounds, or he will kill you."

The old merchant started to his feet so quickly, that Corralli drew back a pace, and laid his hand upon his knife. " A hundred thousand grandmothers ! Did any one ever hear of such a sum except in the Bank cellars ! If you were to sell me up to-morrow, I could not command the half of it. I will not give him a hundred thousand pence."

" Ay, the bank," put in Corralli cunningly, again recognising a scrap of what was said ; " now that is like coming to business. He is talking of Gordon's bank at Palermo, is he not? That is, of course, where the money will come from."

" Indeed, he is talking of nothing of the kind," said Walter calmly. The excitement of the merchant, which had certainly testified to the extravagance of the demand as strongly as any words could have done, had not, as he fancied, been thrown away upon the brigand chief. " He was saying that no private person, even in England, could command such a sum as you propose. He has not got it to give, nor yet the half of it."

" Then, by Santa Rosalia, he shall die !" cried the brigand, " and you along with him."

" It may be so, Captain Corralli, for it lies within your power to kill us——"

" Ay, and to do more, look you—to roast you, to skin you !"

" Just so ; you mentioned all that before.

It is in your power to do anything to us that you are wicked enough to imagine; but it is not in this man's power to pay the sum you propose. We shall die sooner or later, at all events—then you will be left, as you say, with our skins—they will not be worth much, and in the end you will be taken, and hanged for it. If you consider such a course of conduct advantageous, you must pursue it. For my part, if I were in your place, I would be a little more reasonable."

The brigand's face was black with rage; he looked more like a vulture than a human being, as he gazed on the unhappy merchant, as though longing to fall on him with beak and claw.

"You do not know me, Signor Inglese, or you would not dare to speak to me thus," said he to Walter. "Are we lawyer and client, that you give me advice of this sort, and cross my will when I have expressed it?"

"I would not cross it if I could help it, Captain Corralli; but your demands are those of a madman, of a man who wishes to have our blood, by demanding of us an impossibility."

"It is possible that you may be speaking the truth," answered Corralli, after a long pause. "If this man has really but three hundred thousand ducats, with that I must be content. But if he does not possess *them*, then let him prepare for death, since, for a less sum, he shall never escape alive out of my hands. And let him come to his conclusion, 'Yea' or 'Nay,' within ten minutes, for my patience has reached its limit." As he said these words the brigand produced one of the various watches that adorned his person—a gold one, encrusted with jewels, the spoil probably of some native milord—and placed it on the ground before him, where it formed a spot of sunshine in that shady place.

Walter translated this ultimatum to the old merchant, and added an expression of his own belief that nothing less than the sum now named would suffice the brigand's greed.

"Fifty thousand pounds!" cried the old man in an agony. "Why, that will be ruin, Mr. Litton—beggary!"

Walter did not believe that this was literally true. It was quite possible that

such a sum was as great as even the merchant's credit could have realized in ready
money so far from home; but it could
surely not be his whole fortune; and in his
heart he wondered how, for an instant, considering the position of Lilian, her father
should have hesitated to give in to terms
that, however hard, were yet practicable.
He did not know how dear is wealth to
those who have much of it, especially when
it has been acquired by their own hands;
how one's ducats and one's daughter, if not
rated at the same value, bear yet some pro-
portion to one another, in such a man's
mind, as they had in that of the Jew of
Venice. Moreover, he did not take into
sufficient account the natural incapacity of
the owner of Willowbank, Regent's Park,
to believe in the menaces of their captor.
Mr. Christopher Brown had probably never
read M. About's "King of the Mountains,"
nor that matchless tale of M. Dumas,
wherein he describes how the banker in the
hands. of brigands is charged a hundred
thousand francs for an egg—a not particu-
larly fresh one—and at a similar rate for all
other necessities of the table, till his bill

for board equals the ransom he has declined to pay; and if he had read them, he would have taken them for romances, as void of foundation as a fairy tale. He was scarcely in fact more capable of realizing his present circumstances, than he would have been of imagining them, if they had not occurred. And though he saw himself fallen among thieves, and wholly in their power, he found it hard to believe that they would venture on such extremities as Walter had fore-shadowed. The London cry, " Where are the police ?" was a sentiment that he could not eradicate from his mind. In this matter the brigand chief (who had doubtless had the opportunity of observing such workings of the mind in others of his captives) had gauged the merchant with considerable accuracy.

" No," persisted Mr. Brown; " let the scoundrel do his worst; his sickle shall never reap all the harvest of my life of honest toil. I will die rather than submit to it."

" Alas, sir, it is not a question of dying, if what we have heard of this man's cruel-ties is true," urged Walter, " but of far worse than death ; and, moreover, it is not your life nor mine that are alone at stake. Consider what your daughter must be enduring, and how every moment of delay and haggling may be fraught with peril to her."

"Consider!" echoed the merchant with irritation. "Do you suppose, then, that she has escaped my consideration? I am only thinking whether she would thank me for saving her, since it must needs be done at such a sacrifice to her of wealth, position, comfort, and all that makes life worth having. Three hundred thousand ducats ! It is monstrous, it is incredible ! Two thousand pounds a year for ever in return for two nights' involuntary lodging upon a mountain-side. I will never give it."

The very force and passion of these protestations, however, suggested to Walter that the merchant was at least wavering in his stubborn resolve.

"The question is, Mr. Brown," observed he with earnestness, "is it within your power to command so vast a sum, or not?"

"I have a good name on 'Change, sir!" answered the other, with an assumption of dignity that at any other time would have been amusing to note; and a good name there is good everywhere else."

"Then, for Heaven's sake, use it!" exclaimed Walter passionately. "Why, if you died, sir, under this man's tortures, and Lilian died"—for in the stress and strain of their common misfortune, he spoke of her thus familiarly, and her father listened without reproof — "what would Lady Selwyn say? Would she thank you because your obstinate resolve had enriched her by the sacrifice of a father and a sister?"

"True, true," answered the old man, as if talking to himself; "all would in that case go to Lotty, which would mean to *him*."

By chance, Walter had hit upon an argument more convincing than any which logic or common-sense could have suggested. "Well, well, Mr. Litton, it is a hard case; but I will be guided by you."

"The ten minutes are over," observed the brigand, taking up his watch, and throwing away the end of the cigar with which he had been beguiling the time. "Has Milord come to his right mind?"

"Mr. Brown will pay the money, Captain Corralli—that is, if so huge a sum can be raised in Palermo upon his credit—on one condition. His daughter must be set at liberty on the spot; indeed, the letter of authorization must be delivered to the banker by her hand. It would otherwise be valueless, since he would conclude it to have been extorted by force."

"That shall be done," answered the brigand quietly; "we have no wish to retain the signora. It is a pleasure to me, I assure you, to reflect that we are to remain good friends. The sooner she is away, doubtless the better for her. Here are pens, ink, and paper for the authorization;" and once more the chief produced from an outside pocket those business materials, which were almost as much the implements of his trade as the knife and the musket.

"My friend must see his daughter before she goes," observed Walter quickly. There was something in the brigand's manner that had aroused his suspicions. Was it not possible that that phrase, "The sooner she is away, doubtless the better for her," implied that she was dying?

"That is impossible," answered Corralli coolly, "since Milord does not speak Sicilian.

No word is allowed to pass between a prisoner about to be released and one who is still retained captive, unless in our own language. The signora will take the authorization—which will be read by a friend of ours who is acquainted with the English tongue—but we must take care that she has no secret instructions. I regret to forbid an interview so naturally agreeable, but the precaution is one which will recommend itself to Milord's good sense."

The Tartar, which had been so visible when Captain Corralli's skin had been scratched, was no longer visible; the wound was healed; he was once more in manner the Chesterfield of brigand chiefs.

"But for all we know, the signora may be——" Walter hesitated; he could not bring himself to speak of Death in connexion with his Lilian—"unfit for travel, too ill to bear the journey; or under that pretence, you may not let her free, after you have promised to do so."

"The signor should remember, that without her personal presence at the banker's, as he has just observed, the ransom could not be obtained," answered Corralli blandly.

"If the assurance of her being alive is all that is required, the signor can see her himself—since you both speak our language—but not Milord."

When this was communicated to Mr. Brown, he did not make the opposition to this harsh announcement that Walter had expected; the fact was, that though he loved his daughter with all the strength of a strong nature, he was singularly free from sentiment as such ; in this matter, as in professional affairs, he looked to the main facts, and provided that he could feel assured that Lilian was safe in her friends' hands, he could forego that parting caress which to some men would have been worth the ransom he was about to pay. Moreover, it must be added, that he conceived that all difficulties in the way of his own freedom would be at once removed, and that the next day, or the one after next at farthest, would see him once more on board the *Sylphide*, never to touch land again until they reached the British soil.

"Go and see her, Mr. Litton," said he. "Give her my fondest love, and tell her how it is that I am debarred from bidding

her good-bye. Bid her hasten matters with
the bankers all she can. Since I must pay
this money, the sooner it is done the better;
and if you can do so without being over-
heard, tell her that large as the sum is
which has been extorted from me, she will
not, nevertheless, have to beg her bread—
do you understand?"

Walter understood very well, though he
wondered greatly how Mr. Brown could
comfort himself with such reflections at
such a time, much more recommend them
to others.

Then the merchant drew out the authorization—he had become quite himself again at
the prospect of a business transaction—in
brief and concise terms. It was unnecessary
to dilate upon his necessitous position, since
all the world of Palermo was by this time
acquainted with it; but he was careful, at
the chief's suggestion, to add, beside the
usual formula, that all the ransom must be
paid in gold. His name was well known to
the bankers, to whom he had been duly
recommended; and there was his son-in-
law, Sir Reginald, to vouch for him. The
general sympathy of the commercial public

and of his fellow-countrymen would doubt-less also be of some advantage in such a crisis; and, upon the whole, he did not doubt that the money—which in London he could have produced in a few hours—would be forthcoming in a day or two at the farthest. He did not comprehend—nor indeed did Walter—that the raising of the money was only one of the difficulties that might interpose between them and freedom.

"There!" said Mr. Brown, when he had signed the document, and the other two had witnessed it; "now I have chopped my arm off, I feel better."

To sign away so huge a sum seemed indeed to him like the lopping away of a limb; but when once it was gone, he wiped it off the books of his mind like a bad debt, and commenced the business of life again, under new conditions.

"And now, gentlemen," said Corralli, who had at once possessed himself of the document, "the sooner we get on with this little business the better for all parties.— Santoro!"

At the sound of his name, Walter's body-guard at once made his appearance; he had decked himself out even more splendidly than before, having been lent some personal ornaments by his friends to go a-wooing with; just as a young lady will sometimes borrow a necklace or a bracelet for a ball from her mother's jewel-case.

"I see," said the captain, addressing his follower with great good-humour, " that you have made up your mind to see Lavocca, and, as it happens, the opportunity now offers itself. The signor here is to be conducted to the cavern."

"The cavern!" exclaimed Santoro, as though he could hardly believe his ears.

"Yes; did I not say so? Colletta and yourself will be answerable as before, for his safety, and he will be entrusted to you two alone. If you have any last words for Milord," added he, addressing Walter, "you had better say them."

"Mr. Brown," said Walter, " I am going. Have you anything to add to what you have already said, as respects your daughter?"

"Nothing but my love and blessing, Mr. Litton. But as respects yourself, I would wish to say, in case anything should happen to either of us ere we meet again, that I am

deeply sensible of the good-will towards me
and mine, which has caused you to share
our misfortune. I confess that I behaved
ill to you at Willowbank, and that my first
impression of your character was the true
one." Walter's only answer was to hold
out his hand, which the other took and
pressed warmly. "You will tell me the
truth about my Lilian," faltered the old
man; "you will conceal nothing from me.
It's uncommon hard, because a man only
speaks his mother-tongue, that he mayn't
say good-bye to his daughter. But after
all, it will be only for a few days, will it?
We shall be on board the yacht again before
the week's out, eh?"

"Indeed, sir, I hope you will," said
Walter earnestly; but since it was Thursday
even then, he doubted it.

"If Lilian gets to Palermo this afternoon,
you see," argued Mr. Brown, "the money
can be collected before night, and sent up
here the first thing in the morning. I
assure you it is not so pleasant sleeping
under these beech-trees, that I should wish
to try it a third time. At all events, I do
trust the people at Gordon's will take care

that we don't spend our Sunday in such society as this," and he pointed to the members of the band, who, with characteristic interest in any excitement, had already gathered round to see Walter and his guards depart upon their expedition. The picture of the honest merchant, as he stood without his leafy tent bidding adieu to him in such sanguine words, and denouncing the unconscious spectators, was fated often to recur to Walter's mind in days to come, with a sad sense of contrast.

CHAPTER II.

THE CAVERN.

WHEN Walter left the camp with his two companions, the sun was high in the heavens, and poured down its rays upon a magnificent landscape of wood and mountain, but one which was without a trace of cultivation; not a road was visible in any direction, nor did they come across any pathway, save such as the goats frequented, and which was used by the sure-footed brigands with equal facility. Lofty as was their position, their route still lay upwards, and the summit of the mountain was still hid from their view to the east and north, in which latter quarter, as Walter supposed, lay the sea. He cast his keen eyes hither and thither in hopes of a landmark, and presently, upon

his right, rose Etna, its crown of snow
shining in the morning light as though it
were one jewel. Colletta, who was walking
behind him, marked the quick direction of
his glance, and called out to his companion,
who instantly stopped, and produced from
his pocket a long shawl. He had a dozen
pockets at least in various parts of his
clothing; some for his jewellery, some for
his food, some for his ammunition; while
the flaps of his shooting-jacket, more volu-
minous than those of an English poacher,
could easily have held not only a hare,
but a goat. Santoro's manner was so stern,
and even truculent, upon exhibiting this
unlooked-for commodity, that for an instant
Walter imagined that he was about to be
strangled *à la Turk*, with a shawl instead of
a bowstring, and he drew back a pace
mechanically.

"It is useless to make resistance," said
Santoro coldly. "We have our orders, and
must obey them; it is necessary that the
signor should be blindfolded."

"Blindfolded!" echoed Walter; the
thought of being shot with his eyes bandaged, suggested by what he had read of

military executions, at once occurring to his mind. "No; you may shoot as I am, and be hanged to you." This was an illogical speech, since, if the brigands had intended to take his life without his seeing them, it was obvious they might have done it fifty times over by simply shooting him from behind; but then the conditions were not favourable for logic.

"We mean you no harm, signor," explained Santoro; "but the captain does not choose that you should know the way to our cavern up yonder," and he pointed eastward with his finger.

"But it isn't in Mount Etna, is it?" inquired Walter, smiling, "or I shall have to walk a long way with my eyes shut."

"That hill yonder is not Etna, signor," returned the brigand calmly; and then with his companion's assistance he proceeded to bind the shawl twice and thrice over the upper part of their prisoner's face, like a turban which has slipped a few inches down. Walter knew that the brigand had lied to him concerning Etna, and made up his mind to detect if possible the direction in which they were about to proceed. But this was at once rendered impossible by the simple precaution which children use in blindman's-buff. They turned him round and round three times ; then each taking an arm, they led him away, at first down hill, probably retracing their steps to confuse him, and then again up hill, till the fatigue and heat incident upon his constrained motion and bandaged head became almost insupportable. At last they came to what appeared to be high level ground, with trees, to judge by the coolness and the breeze upon it, and here they halted. Then the brigand call was given, and returned, as it seemed, from close at hand : a few minutes of waiting, during which he heard a grinding noise, as of stone on stone, and then he was bidden to stoop his head and follow Santoro, who guided him by his hand. Half-a-dozen paces of cautious walking, during which his disengaged fingers were bruised against what seemed a rocky passage ; the grinding noise was heard again, and then a wave of cool salt air broke gratefully upon his mouth and cheek. Santoro had let go his hand, so that he dared not move, since, for aught he knew, he was at the summit of some dizzy precipice; but if his sense of hearing could be trusted, there was a woman's cry of welcome, and then kisses. These lasted for a considerable interval, during which he stood with bowed head and blinded eyes, doubtless in a very ridiculous position; then a woman's smothered laugh broke tinkling out, and Santoro cried: "A thousand pardons, signor; I had quite forgotten that you were still stooping: you can now hold up your head."

"But can I take off the bandage?"

"In one moment, signor;" but there was more kissing, and a whispered word or two, and a sound like a slapped cheek, before the shawl was loosened and he was permitted to look about him.

The scene that saluted Walter's dazzled eyes was very surprising. He found himself in a vast cavern, the arch of which, so far from endangering his head, was fifty feet above it; huge stalactites, on which the sunbeams shone, and gave to them the brightness of lit chandeliers, depended from the roof; while the sides of the cave, notwithstanding it was warm and dry, were

lined with luxuriant creepers. The floor,
a sparkling sand, which would have com-
peted with salt for whiteness, was soft and
noiseless to the feet as thick-piled carpet.
Of windows this noble chamber could not
boast; but through a vast natural opening—
by which the light and air were at present
freely admitted, but could be excluded at
will by a mat-curtain—the blue sea could
be seen far as eye could reach. The sight
of it was almost like liberty itself to Walter,
and for an instant his gaze rested on it with
thankful joy, to the neglect of other objects;
then it lit on a young lad, more smartly
dressed than any of his late companions on
the mountain, but the knife and pistol in
whose belt proclaimed him to follow the
same lawless trade; he leant against the
opposite wall, with his eyes fixed on the
sand, and was apparently unconscious of a
stranger's presence.

"Why, where is Santoro gone," inquired
Walter, "and—and—the lady?"

"Santoro will return in a moment,
signor," murmured the lad. The soft
gentle voice struck Walter as familiar, but
it was the tell-tale blush upon the cheek,

and the shy glance of the eye, which disclosed to him that he was addressing a female.

" Oh, I see," cried he with some awkwardness ; " you are Lavocca."

" Yes, signor." He wondered now how, despite her brigand attire, he could have ever taken her for a boy, so feminine were her looks and tone. It was evident that the mention of her name had revealed to her that he was acquainted with Santoro's love for her, and that the knowledge overwhelmed her with confusion. She stood swaying her foot upon the sand, and playing with the pistol in her dainty sash, as though it had been a flower which she would have picked to pieces. For a Sicilian she was almost a blonde, and a very pretty one ; her hair curled in profusion about her ears and temples, but descended no lower, forbidden doubtless, to do so by the brigand code ; her mouth, though weak in its expression, was a very charming one, and no man who desired to be her husband would probably have wished it stronger.

" But what on earth has become of Santoro ?" repeated Walter with curiosity.

"His fingers untied this shawl but one minute ago, and now he has vanished."

"He is here," said Lavocca, interrupting, "and the young signora with him."

"The signora!" cried Walter, turning eagerly round, and expecting to behold no other than Lilian herself.

"That is the name by which my people honour me," said a grave sweet voice; "but I am plain Joanna, sister of Rocco Corralli, at your service."

The speaker was a tall and strikingly handsome girl—so tall, that even in her male costume her height did not appear insignificant. Her hair, which was quite short and straight, except for a tiny curl at each ear, which had a charming effect, was black and glossy as a crow's wing; her eyes were also black as blackest coal, and though mild and maidenly in their present expression, could perhaps, like coal, give forth flame upon occasion; while her complexion, which had once doubtless been olive, like that of the majority of her fellow-countrywomen, had become by exposure to the sun and wind of a deep walnut. In woman's clothes she would probably have looked coarse, but in her jacket braided with silver buttons, and tied at the waist with a rich scarlet scarf, her full trousers of blue cloth, and small though thick-soled boots, she was as bewitching a figure as ever stepped before the footlights.

It was not in the young painter's nature to have refused admiration to so picturesque an object, and besides he reflected that Lilian was in this woman's power, and that it behoved him to conciliate her by all the arts he knew. I am afraid therefore that he affected to be even more struck by this lady's appearance than he really was, and allowed a certain respectful homage to be perceived in his looks and tone as he addressed her, which were not wholly genuine.

"I am come, signora, from your brother, with a message to the young lady under your protection, as Santoro here" (for the brigand had returned with Joanna) "has doubtless informed you."

"Is she a relative of yours?" inquired Joanna in a careless tone, but with a certain quickness of manner that did not escape Walter's notice. He was no coxcomb, but if his appearance had made a favourable impression upon this Amazon, it was his interest—and that of another—to improve it.

" No, signora."

" Oh, indeed. Then may I ask how it happens that you have been sent hither instead of her father?"

" Well, for one thing, Mr. Brown could only speak English; and it seems that it is contrary to your custom to allow a prisoner who is about to leave you——"

" How do you know she is about to leave us? I mean, how did my brother know?" interrupted Joanna haughtily. " The lady is in my hands, not his."

" I know nothing of that, signora," answered Walter deferentially, " being, alas, but a captive myself. I am ·only your brother's mouthpiece. A very large sum has been agreed upon as our ransom, and, that cannot be procured unless the young lady applies to the banker in person. I understood, too, that she was far from well, and to an invalid—however admirably such quarters may agree, as one can see they do with one like yourself, in health—these open-air lodgings must needs be hurtful."

" The young lady is well lodged enough, as you shall presently see for yourself," answered Joanna : " the air that is here admitted so freely " — and she stepped towards the orifice of the cave, while Lavocca gave place to her, and stole to where Santoro was standing, at the other end of the apartment—" is shut out from our inner room. And what was the other reason which you were about to say brought you here?" continued Joanna, dropping her voice, so that Walter alone could hear her. " Was it curiosity to behold, before you returned to your friends, a woman outlawed and unsexed ; the companion, and even the leader, of outlaws ; one who, while still a girl in years, had forgotten not only how to love, but how to pity ?" The words were spoken with bitterness, but the look that accompanied the words was far from bitter ; it was remonstrant, and almost pleading.

" Indeed, signora, you misjudge me : it was no mere curiosity that brought me here ; and if it had been so, I should have expected to see no such being as you describe, for I have heard no such account of her."

"Then what sort of person did you expect to see?"

"A young girl, whom the tyranny of circumstances had driven to a mode of life that is indeed to be deplored, but who, while embracing it, has given proofs of kindness and generosity, which would have adorned a far more enviable position."

"Your informant," answered Joanna, sighing, but evidently greatly pleased, "must, I am afraid, have been Santoro yonder, who has his special reasons, as we see, for currying favour with the mistress of Lavocca."

"He could not have known that I should quote him, signora, since I heard his account of you long before my coming here was arranged. I am well convinced, since the face is the index of the mind, that his praise was well deserved."

"Ah, signor, you have not seen me in one of my passions," said Joanna naïvely. "We Sicilians are not like your English misses—so quiet, so gentle, like that one in yonder room. But I perceive you are impatient to see her. Come with me, sir."

Joanna's voice had suddenly altered; her

tones, which had been almost tender, became cold and stern. Her very figure had changed; for, whereas she had been leaning against the curtain, and partly hidden in the shadow of it, in an attitude of graceful ease, she now drew herself up, like a soldier on parade, and led the way across the cavern with quick determined tread.

Close behind where Santoro and Lavocca were now standing in earnest but low-toned talk, and where Walter himself had stood, till, at a sign from Joanna, he had changed his place, was a sort of recess in the wall of the cave: it was dark, and apparently of small extent, but at the touch of Walter's companion, what seemed to be rock, but was in fact a door, rudely painted in imitation of it, opened without noise, and revealed a second apartment, smaller than the first, but furnished like an ordinary room. There were chairs and a table in it; a thick carpet covered the floor; instead of plants and ferns, the walls were hung with the same kind of matting of which the curtain in the outer cave had been composed. It was lighted, like its fellow, by an orifice that looked seaward, but to west instead of north, and which could be closed at pleasure by a wooden shutter. Close beside it, and yet sheltered from the draught, was a rude couch, covered with rugs and cushions, upon which lay a female form.

" The young lady is asleep," said Joanna softly.

Walter's limbs trembled beneath him, as he bent down to gaze upon the unhappy Lilian. Her eyes were closed, but there were traces of tears upon her pale cheek, in the centre of which there burned a hectic spot of fever; he could hardly recognise her for even the invalid he had seen carried up and down the Marina. " Great Heaven, how ill she looks!" was his smothered ejaculation.

" She has suffered from alarm and fatigue," observed Joanna coldly; " she has been distressed too about the safety of her friends. It will doubtless do her good to see you."

" Would you be kind enough to break it to her that I am here?" said Walter, stepping back a pace. " She is not aware that I have been taken captive, nor even of my presence in Sicily. The sudden shock might do her harm."

"One is not killed by unexpected happiness," returned Joanna, "or at least so I have been told by those who have experienced it; but nevertheless I will do your bidding. Who shall I say has come? You are not a relative, it seems. Shall I say that it is her betrothed?"

"I am not her betrothed," answered Walter gravely.

"But you hope to be so," returned the other quickly. "I read it in your face."

"Indeed, I have no hope of the sort, signora," was Walter's calm reply. He did not feel it necessary to explain to her why he had none; but he had spoken the literal truth. Not only was the difference of their fortunes as insurmountable as heretofore (for he was well convinced that Mr. Brown could pay his ransom and yet remain a wealthy man), but there was that in Lilian's look which foreshadowed to him that she would live to be the bride of no man. "I am her friend, and her father's friend, and that is all. My name is Walter Litton."

Joanna approached the couch, and placed her hand softly upon Lilian's own. She awoke at once with a start.

" Is papa here ?" cried she excitedly.

" Your father is not here, but a friend has come to see you."

" A friend ?   Alas ! I have no friend except my father."

" He calls himself so, at all events; he has brought some news for you, but you must not talk of it in English, else you cannot see him."

" In English !   Is he then an Englishman ?"

" Yes; his name is Walter Litton."

" Walter !"   A low weak cry, in which surprise and tenderness were strangely mingled, escaped her pale lips.

" I am here, Lilian," said Walter, coming forward, and holding out his hand.   " Do not excite yourself; I bring you good tidings."

" But how came you here ?" She retained his hand in hers, but closed her eyes after one glance of grateful recognition.

" It is a long story, which there is no time to tell you now.   Let it suffice that I have been taken captive with your father."

" Ah, you risked then your life for mine."   These words came from the heart, and like the rest were spoken in her native tongue.

"You must not speak English," broke in Joanna.

"Pardon her, signora; it will not occur again," said Walter. "She fears that her father's life is menaced. No, Lilian; he will regain his liberty, if only the ransom which he has agreed to give can be procured. The authorization for its payment, which you will present at Gordon's bank, is here"— he placed it in her hand. "When once the money has been received, he will be free."

"And you?" In those two words were expressed all the tenderest emotions of which a woman's heart is capable. Walter felt that she was aware at once of all that he had believed, contrived, and endured for her sake, from the moment of their last parting.

"I shall be free also in a day or two, at furthest; when we shall be sent back in safety to Palermo. Our only anxiety is, indeed, upon your account. Do not fret yourself as respects us. It is the thought of your condition—the trials, the hardships to which you have been exposed—that wrings your father's heart. Do you feel that you have strength enough to return to the city, where your sister's loving tendance awaits you?—Signora," here he turned to Joanna—"you said something awhile ago of this poor lady being your prisoner, to be dealt with according to your own good pleasure; but I am well convinced that you will not refuse your brother's wish that she should be set free at once. You see how weak and ill she is. To keep her here would be to kill her."

"And what then?" whispered Joanna in his ear.

"Why, then I should say that what some folks have said of you (as you told me) was only too true: that you were a woman unsexed, and without a heart."

"You would be wrong," answered she, in the same low tones, but without the harshness that had accompanied her previous words. "Even if I acted as you suggest, I should have a justification. This girl is nothing to me, nay, perhaps worse than nothing. Still, for your sake," here her voice became soft and musical, "all shall be as you wish; she shall be carried to Palermo this very day."

"Lilian," cried Walter joyfully, "the signora has promised to set you free at once; before to-night you will be clasped in your sister's arms! Let that thought give you strength and courage."

"I will do my best, Walter," answered Lilian feebly; "but my brain seems on fire, and my limbs do not obey my will."

"You hear her, signora!" pleaded Walter passionately. "Oh, do not let a minute be lost in sending her where aid can be given to her!"

Joanna bowed her head, and glided from the room.

"I shall never see you more, Walter," whispered Lilian.

"Yes, dearest, yes, you will," answered he, falling on his knees beside her; "we shall meet again, and you will once more be well and happy. Hush! she is returning."

At that moment Joanna entered, accompanied by Santoro and Lavocca. These two took up the couch, which was indeed but a litter upon trestles, and carried Lilian forth into the outer room. Walter would have followed, but Joanna made a sign to him to remain.

"You must stay here, signor," said she authoritatively, "or you would learn the secret of finding your way out of prison."

"I have no desire to learn it," answered he, truly enough, since his escape at such a time would probably have endangered the merchant's life.

"Ah, you are smooth of speech, Signor Inglese, but I mistrust such gallantry. You have deceived me once already."

"Not willingly, signora; nor am I conscious of having done so."

"What! not when you told me that you were not betrothed to that young girl, but only her father's friend! Is it usual then in your country for such 'friends' to take leave of one another with kisses?"

"It is allowable," answered Walter with solemnity, "when we believe that we shall never see one another on earth again."

"To be sure, that makes a difference," observed Joanna thoughtfully. "And I certainly agree with you that it is not probable that the young lady will be long-lived."

To this Walter answered nothing, for indeed to him it had seemed as though Lilian's motionless and almost inanimate form had been carried out but to be placed in a still narrower prison-house. He drew a chair to the table, and placing his elbows upon it, covered his face with his hands.

"You would be left alone with your grief, Signor Litton?" said Joanna interrogatively, and laying her hand upon the door.

"Thank you, yes," answered he, scarcely knowing what he said.

"Those are his first thanks," observed she bitterly, as she left the room; "thanks for my absence." But if Walter heard her words, he did not heed them; he was picturing to himself the English burial-ground at Palermo, as he had seen it a few days ago, and wondering in what part of its beautiful garden-ground they would lay his Lilian.

CHAPTER III.

JOANNA.

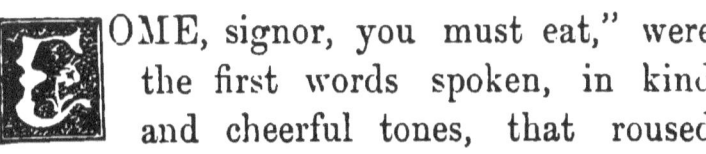

OME, signor, you must eat," were the first words spoken, in kind and cheerful tones, that roused Walter from the stupor of sorrow into which Lilian's departure under such sad conditions had cast him. Joanna was standing by him, with a loaf of bread in one hand, and a bottle of wine in the other; she placed these upon the table, and then produced from a cupboard some cold kid and a pot of cream. This solicitude for his comfort did not fail to move the young fellow towards her. The hearts of all his sex are approachable through the palate, and in this case Walter had every excuse for giving way to human weakness, for he was exceedingly hungry; moreover, he was not so imprudent as not to perceive the immense importance of making friends with the sister of the brigand chief; so he fell to on the viands with honest vigour.

"Have they starved you up in the mountains yonder?" inquired she, watching him with pleased surprise.

"They have not treated me so well as you do, signora. Allow me to congratulate you upon the contents of your cellar. Why, this is more like a liqueur than a wine!"

"It is *lacrymæ Christi*. The mayor of the village hereabouts is good enough to send us some at Easter-tide."

"To *send* us some!" thought Walter, and he felt as the Black Knight might have done, had he been more conscientious, when the friar of Copmanhurst described how he got his venison.

"Do not imagine it is stolen," laughed Joanna, reading his thoughts; "we brigands are not the outlaws that you are inclined to imagine us. We have friends in higher places than you imagine; and as for the poor—when did you ever hear us spoken ill of by a poor man?"

Walter thought of his host on the Marina,

confined to a few square miles of ground for
life because of Captain Corralli and Company, but he remained silent.

" I see you are determined to think ill of
us," said Joanna plaintively.

" I think ill of the trade, signora, I confess.   See what it has done in my case."

" Your 'friend,' the young lady, was
ailing before she fell into our hands," put
in his companion quickly.

" I was not referring to her, signora, but
to myself.   Here am I—without any fault
of my own, unless the being on a high road
at midnight is a fault—taken prisoner, and
put in danger of my life——"

" I hope not : indeed, I could not smile
if I thought it probable," interrupted
Joanna.   " You will pay some money, the
loss of which you will not feel, and will then
be sent back again to your friends.   Your few
days of captivity will be an experience with
which to entertain them, and amongst other
things you will have to tell them is the
account of how you met a horrid female
creature in men's clothes, who lived in a
cavern, and had no heart."

" Indeed, Joanna" (he had unconsciously

dropped the " signora"), I shall always speak
of that incident in quite another way.   It is
no flattery to you to say that the only pleasant
thing that has happened to me during my
captivity has been my reception here ; your
abode and surroundings are a romance in
themselves, the interest of which will not
easily wear away ; your unlooked-for kindness and hospitality I shall never forget ;
the only thing which distresses me about it
is, that you, seeing what you might be,
should be what you are."

" I don't understand you, signor," cried
Joanna, her dark eyes glowing with sudden
fire.

" Nay, I meant no offence ; but to me it
appears deplorable that one so fitted to
adorn an honest home, beautiful enough for
a princess, sound-hearted, generous——"

" That is because I let the signora go,"
observed Joanna bitterly.

" No, indeed ; that only showed you to
be womanly.   To have retained her would
have been cruel, and cruelty is not your
nature.   I say that it seems to me that, in
leading the life you do, you throw yourself
away ; and in a little while, when the

excitement of such a mode of existence begins to flag, you will bitterly repent your choice of it."

" I had no choice," said Joanna sullenly.

" You have it now, signora. When this unhappy business is over, you have only to come into Palermo, and I will answer for it that you have made a friend there who will provide for you a better future."

" And who is that friend?" inquired Joanna, with her eyes fixed upon the ground.

" The young lady whom you have just set free: she has a grateful heart, and her father is a man of wealth."

" I do not wish to be indebted to that young lady," answered Joanna coldly. " I would rather be a brigand than a beggar, in any case; and never would I beg of her. Let us cease to talk of my affairs, signor; they may appear to interest you now, but they will not do so a week hence. The memory of all your sex is very short; but that of a rich man like you for a poor girl like me—bah! he only thinks of her while he sees her."

" You are making several mistakes at

once, Joanna," said Walter gravely. "In the first place, I am as poor as you are, probably poorer. I should be totally unable to pay even the small sum your brother fixed upon as the price of my freedom, but that he has permitted Mr. Brown's ransom to cover mine."

"You are, however, the betrothed of this rich man's daughter."

"I again declare to you that such is not the fact; my poverty would, in any case, forbid such an alliance. I am but a penniless painter; this sketch-book is my chequebook, and Nature the only bank from which I draw my income."

"Is this really true, sir?" asked Joanna, regarding him with a steady gaze.

"Do I look so false that it is impossible to believe my words?" returned Walter, smiling.

"O no; you look true enough; and you take no vows to the saints, which is also a good sign," answered Joanna naïvely; "but still I cannot believe you. An Englishman, and poor! That is incredible."

"And yet there are a good many of them

in that condition, I do assure you," said Walter, smiling.

" Well, let me prove you. You say you are an artist—one who makes his living by his pencil; if it be so, draw *me*."

" With the greatest pleasure, signora."

" Do not fear that it will be lost time," continued she eagerly; " I have plenty of ducats."

" Nay, nay; I will not take your portrait except for love—that is, for nothing."

" What! you call love nothing?"

" No, indeed; that is only our English phrase. The light here, however, is not so good for drawing as in the other apartment. Let us go in there."

She led the way at once into the larger chamber, which was empty.

" Ah! this is kind of you," continued Walter. " You have allowed Lavocca to accompany your late captive on her journey."

" I thought it would please you that she should have a female escort as far as the next village," replied Joanna. " My four men are her bearers, so you have only to kill me to obtain your freedom."

" But in the meantime you have only to shoot me with one of your pistols."

" No, Signor Litton," answered his companion softly, " I have never shot any one yet, and your blood, of all men's, will certainly never stain my hands. You can kill me still, as far as my pistols are concerned," and with a sudden impulse she drew them from her girdle, and placed them on the ground at Walter's feet.

" But how would your death avail me ?" argued he, smiling. " If I were to murder you—which Heaven forbid !--I should still be a prisoner, since I do not know the secret of how to leave this enchanted castle."

" To be sure ; I had forgotten that. You shall never say that I did not trust you. See here." She picked up a small crowbar that lay at her feet, and placed it in a crevice of the wall of rock ; at the touch of it, one of the huge stones of which it was composed turned noiselessly inwards, revealing a dark, low-roofed passage. " Stoop your head, signor, and follow me."

Walter obeyed her, and in a few steps found himself in another cave, having a small opening inland.

"Every one knows of this cavern," said Joanna, quietly; "but of the two inner ones no one knows, save half-a-dozen persons. If my brother found that I had disclosed them to you, he would shoot me without mercy. I have therefore placed my life in your hands, and also your own liberty. And now," added she with passionate energy, "that pathway through the wood leads to the high-road to Palermo. Take it if it so please you, and leave me to my fate. Rocco will kill me, to be sure; but you will be happy."

"Nay, Joanna, in that case I should certainly not be happy," answered Walter soothingly. "Nor do you think so ill of me as to believe it."

"Alas! I do not think ill of you," sighed Joanna; "and I wish you would think less ill of me." Her voice had sunk very low, and her words were almost inaudible to Walter, whom the fresh air and the sense of the opportunity of freedom (though he had no idea of taking advantage of it) was filling with unwonted pleasure.

"And how far is it from hence to Palermo?" inquired he thoughtfully.

"Not ten miles. You could reach it on foot within three hours; nor would there be any chance of falling in with my brother's men upon the road."

Walter had not asked the question with any reference to himself, but with the view of hearing how soon Lilian might be expected to reach the city; but he had the prudence to conceal this. "It is strange, Joanna," said he rebukefully, "that you, who have shown such a generous confidence, should give no credit to others for even the commonest gratitude. Come, let us go within, lest those who are more jealous of your captive's safety than yourself should return and find him outside his cage."

As they retraced their steps, Joanna showed him how the inner chambers of this subterranean home were reached. The exterior cavern had nothing remarkable about it, and indeed had at one time been used as a cow-house by the neighbouring shepherds. Any explorer would naturally

have given his attention to its extremity,
but it was immediately at the entrance, on
the right-hand side, that the moveable stone
was situated; this turned, as it were, upon
a pivot, the natural mechanism of which
had been assisted by art, and required from
without nothing but a gentle pressure to
set it in motion.

"You do not regret having confided to
me this secret, Joanna?" inquired Walter,
as, pencil in hand, he watched her face,
preparatory to transferring it to his sketch-
book, and noticed how suddenly it had
grown pale and grave.

"No; I think not. I am certain you
will not betray us. But, in my desire to
show I trusted you, I forgot that I was im-
perilling the safety of others as well as my
own. To some men—poor as you describe
yourself to be—this knowledge would have
been a great temptation, since it might any
day produce them twelve thousand ducats."

"How so?"

"Because that is the sum that is set
upon my brother's head—and this cavern,
when he is closely pursued, is his hiding-
place."

"Well, I am not so poor as to take blood-money," answered Walter smiling. "Your secret is as safe with me, Joanna, as though it had never been revealed: there is my hand upon it."

She took it, carried it to her lips, and then retained it. It was an embarrassing position for any young gentleman, not enamoured of the lady, this demonstration; and especially so, when he wanted the use of his fingers to take her portrait. Perhaps Walter would not have been so hard-hearted, had he not just parted from his Lilian, ill, perhaps dying, and whose last kiss was still lingering on his cheek; but, as it was, he gently withdrew his hand, and commenced his picture.

Under other circumstances it would have been a task very congenial to him; for never had painter a sitter more picturesque than his present one. Joanna's charms, striking as they were at first sight, were (unlike those of dark beauties in general) even more attractive the longer the eye rested on them. Her black eyes, when in repose, as now, had a certain blueness in them, not cold, like that of the sloe,

but warm and tender; at the same time,
her face wore a certain dignity, for which
women are, in general, compelled to use
haughtiness as the substitute. Her male
attire from long custom, was worn without
awkwardness, and became her grandly; and
there were freedom and grace in every
movement, when at the artist's request, she
changed the position of a limb. He had
been drawing for only a few minutes, when
suddenly the shrill moist note with which
Walter's ear had become familiar, was
heard without; and she instantly started to
her feet. "Away, into the other room!"
cried she.

Walter understood that this was lest he
should appear to be a witness to the
opening of the secret door, and hastened to
obey her. "Santoro and the others have
returned I suppose?"

"Hush! no," said she pushing him
quickly out; "it is Rocco."

Hardly had he time to gain the inner
apartment, when the stone revolved upon
its pivot, and Corralli sprang into the room
Walter had just quitted.

The attire of the brigand chief was torn

and stained with blood; his face scarlet
with haste and anger, or both, and covered
with perspiration.

"Where are the Englishman and the
girl?" were his first impatient words.

"The Englishman is in yonder. The
girl has been sent to Palermo, at your
request, as Santoro informed me."

"Let her be followed, and brought back
at once."

"There is no one to do it; all the men
went away with her, since she had to be
carried on a litter. She is ill; and indeed,
as I think, dying."

"No matter; she shall die with us, not
with her friends. People will say else that
we gave her up through fear. The troops
have fired upon us, as if that were the way
to treat with me and mine. I will have her
back, alive or dead. How long is it since
she left you?"

"More than three hours," answered
Joanna calmly.

It had not, in fact, been half that time,
as Walter, whom not a word of this conversation escaped, though it was not all intelli-
gible to him, was well aware.

" Il diavolo !" muttered the brigand, striking his heel into the sand of the cavern. " It will be the worse for those that are left. Where is this fellow ?" Then he strode into the inner room, and confronted Walter.

" Look you," cried he passionately, " you think all is well with you, because this old man's daughter has escaped from me. But you will find, unless she sends the money before the week is out, that all is not so well. There are some things that are sweeter than money. These soldiers of yours have done us a mischief, and somebody shall pay for it. Do you understand me ?"

" Indeed, Captain Corralli, it is easy to understand that something has put you out of temper," answered Walter calmly. " But if the soldiers have attacked you, it is at least plain that neither Mr. Brown nor I could have sent them."

" They came on your account, however ; and what has happened goes down to your account. Bind his eyes, Joanna."

" What is it you are about to do, Rocco?" inquired the girl with hesitation.

"To take him away with me at once, lest another bird should slip out of the cage."

"But he is surely safer here than any-where," urged Joanna.

"Do as I bid you, or I will make him safe enough at once!" and the brigand touched one of the pistols in his belt. "Now, fasten his arms behind him."

"An impediment to your movements, brother."

"Tush! Do you suppose that I am going to give him a chance of tripping me over a precipice. He will go fast enough with my knife behind him, I'll warrant."

"What! are you going alone with him? Hark! there is the signal. Santoro and the rest will have returned."

"So much the better for this gentleman here," grunted the brigand, "since he will have his arms loose. Otherwise, I should have waited for none of them. I am not in a mood to be trifled with, Mr. English-man. It will be a word and a pistol-shot to-day with you, if you do not step out."

"Don't answer him," whispered Joanna, in

Walter's ear. "He has spilt blood to-day, and is dangerous."

The speech and manner of the captain were, indeed, like those of a madman. No sooner had those who had formed Lilian's escort entered the cavern, than they were ordered on the march, though two of them at least had done a good day's work in that way already. No other voice was heard save that of the furious chief; but as Walter, with blinded eyes, was quitting the cavern, he felt a parcel placed in the pocket of his shooting-coat, and the pressure of a soft hand, that seemed to bid him be of good courage.

CHAPTER IV.

HARD TIMES.

OR a long time Walter walked on in darkness, painfully stumbling as his companions moved rapidly along, notwithstanding that two of them kept close beside him and held him by the arms, as before. He believed them to be Santoro and Colletta, but not a word was now spoken by any one, even Corralli himself. At the expiration of about an hour, the bandage was removed from the captive's eyes, and he found himself in a locality that was altogether strange to him. The sea had disappeared, nor could the white summit of Etna be seen in the distance, as when he had last looked forth ; but he knew by the direction of the sun that they were marching towards that mountain, that is, to the south-east. The way was steep and difficult, to which circumstance, rather than to any mercy upon the captain's part, he attributed the removal of the bandage. There was no mercy to be read in the blood-shot eyes of the brigand chief, which roved hither and thither, more like those of a wild beast in search of prey, than of one who was beset by hunters. At times he would stop for a few seconds to sweep the landscape with his spy-glass, but otherwise there was no halt. Now plunging down steep ravines; now clinging to the sides of sheer precipices, upon a path on which there was room for but one foot to tread; now pushing through tangled scrub; now leaping from rock to rock across brawling torrents, they hurried on. Yet the brigands showed no signs of fatigue. Walter could not but admire the unrelaxing vigour of their strides, and the indifference with which the various obstacles to their progress were met and surmounted. He had long ago given up his first opinion as to their want of activity, but it seemed to him now that their muscles must be made of iron. Pride alone, dislike to own himself, as an Englishman, vanquished in athletics

by men of a race whom he had always held
to be indolent and effeminate, prevented
him from throwing himself on the ground,
and demanding at all risks a respite from
this unceasing toil, while Santoro, a man
nearly double his age, and who had had an
extra journey that morning as one of the
bearers of Lilian's litter, strode on without
a murmur by his side. To add to the
difficulties of their forced march, the rain
had begun to fall so fast and thick, that
it not only wetted them to the skin in spite
of their capotes, but made the cliff paths
slippery and dangerous, besides shutting
out the view beyond a few feet before them.
To fall down some abyss seemed as likely
as not to be Walter's fate, whose footsteps
had become unnerved, and whose eyes were
failing him ; nor, in his desperate condition,
did the prospect appear otherwise than
welcome.   Presently, as they descended into
a little dell, up the other side of which he
felt that his limbs could scarcely carry him,
a small thin column of smoke was seen
rising from the opposite bank. A halt was
called at once, and the two men who had
had charge of the cavern were sent forward

to reconnoitre. Instead of returning, the brigand call was heard from the place where they had disappeared, and for the first time upon Corralli's face there appeared a look of satisfaction. Even this, however, did not last long, for on their ascending the little hill, where, huddling around a scanty fire, were found the remainder of the brigand forces, he broke out into passionate objurgations at their imprudence, and rushing at the cherished flame, extinguished it by standing on it with his feet. At this spectacle, a smothered murmur of disapproval ran round the band.

"What!" cried he, "do you prefer, then, to be shot like Amalli, or taken ·prisoner like Manfred and Duano, rather than to suffer a little cold and damp? Suppose it had been the soldiers instead of ourselves who had discovered you here?"

There was no reply; his logic was indisputable; but the rain was also descending in a continued stream, and anything more wretched than the appearance of the whole party it would have been hard to imagine. The camp, from which, as it seemed, the brigands had been driven out by the troops that morning, had been a paradise compared with their present place of refuge. It was indeed, now that the smoke had ceased, concealed from observation by a circle of stunted shrubs; but those were of no avail to keep off the sheets of rain, nor the wind, which blew in furious gusts, straight from the snow-topped hills to eastward; the turf on which each man lay stretched was sodden with wet; nor was there a sign of either meat or drink to be seen among them. The sheep and goats had evidently fallen into the hands of the soldiers; nor had there been time to secure so much as a leg of mutton or a morsel of kid.

"Have you brought bread with you, captain?" inquired Corbara sulkily.

"I have brought what I went for," answered Corralli frowning, and pointing to Walter. "If you are very hungry, perhaps he may serve instead of bread."

The captain spoke in bitter scorn; but Walter remembered with a shudder that among the frightful crimes he had heard imputed to this man, that of eating human flesh had been included. It was true that this had been done, not from hunger, but revenge : a shepherd, who had been pressed into the service of the troops to point out his hiding-place, having fallen into his hands, he had killed him, and broiled some of his flesh ; but the recollection of this, joined to Corralli's grim reply, was indeed appalling.

" Where is the other prisoner—the English Milord ?" inquired Corralli sternly.

" We have put him under shelter," answered Corbara, " in a hole in the bank yonder."

" You mean to say, you grudged him his share of your fire," replied the captain contemptuously. " But who is guarding him ?"

" Oh, he is safe enough. The fact is, in order the better to keep him warm, and at the same time to make sure of his remaining where he was, we put a rope round him."

" If he has come to harm, your life shall pay for it!" exclaimed Corralli passionately, and striding hastily towards the place the other had indicated. Walter followed, Santoro and Colletta, his shadows, moved, perhaps, by an impulse of curiosity, permitting him so to do, and, of course, accompanying him. The spectacle he beheld would have been ludicrous, had it not been so pitiful. In a hollow space at the foot of a thorn-tree, from which the wet earth had fallen away, and into which he exactly fitted, lay, swathed from head to foot in a sheepskin, like a mummy or an Indian child, the unhappy form of the British merchant.

" Why, they have trussed the man like a fowl !" ejaculated Corralli.

" Have you brought me a fowl ?" cried Mr. Brown eagerly, his knowledge of the Sicilian tongue, sharpened by appetite, enabling him to comprehend that single word.

" No, Milord Inglese; nor is it likely you will taste one in this life, unless your ransom reaches my hands pretty quickly."

" At least you can cut his bonds," pleaded Walter, " even if you cannot give him food. Such cruelty will not bring your ducats a moment earlier."

" Do you call this cruelty ?" answered Corralli savagely. " Ah, by Heaven, in a day or two, if the gold does not come, you

shall see what you shall see! In the meantime, however, as you say, the man may
scratch himself if he has a mind;" and
drawing his knife, he stooped down, and
with two slashes—which showed the opera-
tion was no novelty—freed the captive from
his bonds. Then for the first time, the poor
merchant, who had been lying flat on his
back, with his face within a few inches of
the wet earth, was enabled to recognise his
fellow-prisoner.

"Ah, Mr. Litton, what news of Lilian?"
were his first words, as he scrambled into a
sitting posture.

"She is in Palermo by this time, and in
safe hands."

"Thank Heaven for that!" cried the old
gentleman fervently. "Is she tolerably
well? Has she been taken care of?"

"She was suffering from the shock of all
she has endured, and from anxiety on your
account; but the women who had charge of
her had done for her what they could."

"Ah, then they are human, it seems—not
like their husbands and brothers," answered
Mr. Brown, with a gesture of disgust.
"Well, well, I must not grumble, since my

darling is safe; but may she never know what I have suffered!"

"Nay; I hope in a few days, you may be able to tell her yourself; when your misfortunes being over, will seem to you to have been less terrible than they now appear."

"Ah, you don't know what I have gone through, sir!" answered the merchant, throwing up his hands. "Nothing has passed my lips, to begin with, since you left me. I have been shot at by a troop of soldiers; dragged up such precipices, as one would have thought only a fly could have kept his feet upon; and pricked with knife-points, until I ventured down them. This wet hole into which they thrust me seemed a couch of down for the first few hours, though I have, doubtless, caught my death in it. And to think, there have been times, when I have fancied my sheets were damp and clamoured for a warming-pan!"

It would indeed have been hardly possible to find a person of the male sex more unfitted to be hurried through a mountainous country in wet weather by a band of brigands, than the unfortunate merchant. He had never perhaps travelled in any rougher description of vehicle than an omnibus in his life, or inhabited any spot where such a convenience was not within call. Of late years—though he had given up his carriage to his daughters—he had scarcely made use of his legs at all; while his surplusage of breath had decreased as his girth had enlarged; and yet there was a certain stubborn courage—a part of the same grit that had caused him to win his way in the world of commerce—which enabled him to wear a better front in presence of his persecutors than might reasonably have been expected. Even his complaints had a droll touch in them, and showed no whining or despairing spirit— that is while Corralli and the two brigands were standing by; but when the chief had withdrawn himself, and the others had removed to a spot nearer to their fellows and yet from which they could exercise the needful supervision over their captives, the old merchant's voice began to tremble. "Yes, these blackguards will see the end of me, Mr. Litton; I can never stand such

another day's march as this has been. If I
was your age, there would be a chance for
me, though I was never fit for much in the
way of walking; but as it is, I would rather
die in this hole here like a rat, than suffer
such fatigue."

Walter was well aware that no such eu-
thanasia as dying like a rat would be
permitted his unfortunate companion, in
case the ransom failed to be paid; but it was
not necessary to inform him of that circumstance. He only expressed his hope that
they would not again be disturbed by the
troops, so as to render another retreat in
face of the enemy necessary.

"In that case, my young friend," answered
Mr. Brown, "it seems to me that we shall
perish of starvation. Nothing, as I say, has
passed my lips—with the trifling exception
of a raw onion—for the last ten hours.
I would give its weight in gold for
a hunch of bread and cheese; or for 'a
sandwich and a glass of ale,' such as they
used to sell in the old days in Holborn for
fourpence. Think of a sandwich and a glass
of ale!"

"I am afraid I can command neither of

those delicacies, Mr. Brown," said Walter; "but I believe I have something in my pocket—a bit of cold kid and a slice of bread, which was given to me by the signora——"

"Who was *she?* No matter; she must have been an angel," interrupted the merchant with vivacity. "I am sure you would not have mentioned it, had you not intended to give me a mouthful or two, eh?" and the old gentleman looked perfectly ghastly in his anxiety.

"My dear sir, you need it more than I, for I had a hearty meal before our march, and therefore you are welcome to the whole of it, such as it is." And Walter proceeded to empty the contents of his pocket into the other's outstretched hand.

"Hush! be careful," whispered the old merchant cunningly, "or those rascals will observe us, and snatch the precious morsel for themselves. Mr. Litton, you're a good fellow; you're a gentleman, you're a Christian! What mutton! Talk of Southdown, talk of Welsh! I don't think I ever tasted such bread! Where do they bake it, I wonder? You must have a bit—just a little bit, even if you don't want it—or I shall feel like a pig."

Walter did want it very much, and he accepted a small piece of what had been his own without apology.

"I know I am greedy," continued Mr. Brown naïvely; "but I have no shame, and that's a fact. I have not had such an appetite since I was so high, and used to put the skid on the omnibuses. The signora, as you call her, didn't happen to give you anything to drink with it, did she?"

"She had no opportunity for that, I'm afraid," said Walter smiling.

"Never mind," said Mr. Brown philosophically; "there's plenty of water—I haven't a dry rag on me—you have only to make a hollow of your hand, and the skies fill it for you. To think that this is the Italian climate some fools are always boasting about!" It was astonishing how a little food had resuscitated the old gentleman. "Come, I drink the signora's health, though in liquid utterly unworthy of her. What did you say her name was?"

"The name of the lady who gave me the bread and meat was Joanna."

" Well, Heaven bless her! I only wish she had given you some more. Here's to Joanna! There is no woman, with the exception of my own daughters, for whom, though I have not the pleasure of knowing her, I have so profound a respect."

" I don't think Mrs. Sheldon would like to hear you say so, sir," observed Walter involuntarily.

" Mrs. Sheldon? I don't care one three-penny-piece for Mrs. Sheldon!" answered the old gentleman tartly. " Why, it was through her advice that I was induced to come into this infernal country. And I don't mind telling you, that you yourself are making a great mistake, if you have any high opinion of that woman. It was she who set me against you at Willowbank, and I believe she told me lies; for a man who will give such mutton and bread as that away, when he does not know when he may get another meal himself, cannot possibly be a bad fellow."

There is no doubt that Mr. Christopher Brown had come to a correct conclusion respecting his young friend; but the reason which had led him to it at last was curious enough, when one considers how many others, and better ones, might have convinced him of it before. The fact is, that human nature, when thrown out of the groove of convention, is very soon reduced to its primary elements. It would probably have taken some time to make a brigand out of this eminent British merchant, because, to become so, he would have had to learn as well as unlearn; but he was very fast returning to the savage, out of which state the self-made man springs, Minerva-like, to the admiration of all who are not personally acquainted with him. Had he fallen amongst a tribe of American Indians, he would probably have become not only acclimatized, but nationalized in a twelvemonth. The knowledge that Walter had lost his liberty in attempting to give aid to himself and Lilian, had evoked in him no such gratitude as the sacrifice had deserved; their position had not then appeared to him so dangerous; and above all, he had personally suffered neither pain nor privations; but now—now that Lilian was safe, and he had nothing to think about but his own wretched condition—the gift of the bread and mutton had appealed to all the feeling that was left in him with irresistible force, and carried his heart by storm. His observation with respect to Mrs. Sheldon was perfectly genuine; he hated the woman as one of those who had induced him to take his ill-fated journey; but also because she had lied to him about Walter Litton, who had not only shared with him his last crust and kid, but offered him the whole of it. If the young fellow had done his best for the next ten years, under the conditions of civilized life, to conciliate Mr. Christopher Brown, he could not possibly have made so much progress with him, as he had done in as many hours—and especially in the last few minutes—under the guardianship of Rocco Corralli. It is probable, that if he had even asked permission to woo his daughter, that the old gentleman would not have refused him, in that moment of gratitude and comparative repletion; but, as Walter felt, and only with too much reason, it was no time to flatter himself with any such hopes, even if other circumstances had admitted of their being entertained. Their position in the brigand camp had become perilous in the extreme. Even if the required ransom should be raised without difficulty, there would be a hundred obstacles to its being paid. The government, as in all such cases, would forbid it; and now the troops had been called out, how was such a sum to reach the camp, when even the brigands themselves had escaped their hands only by the greatest exertions? That it would take time to do so, was certain in any case; a time of hardship and privation, such as one of the age and habits of Mr. Brown was very ill fitted to endure; and, above all, was it likely that a man of the temper of the brigand chief would give them time? It was much more probable that, in some moment of impatient fury, he would take his vengeance upon them both, and throwing interest to the winds, gratify a nature to which cruelty was at least as attractive as avarice.

CHAPTER V.

ON PAROLE.

THE apprehensions of Walter respecting the future fate of himself and his companion were, happily for the latter, by no means shared by Mr. Brown. Even when made to understand that there would be some difficulty in getting the ransom into the hands of Corralli, he could not conceive but that he would be willing to wait for days, and even weeks, for a sum that must needs appear to him indeed "beyond the dreams of avarice," and which he himself had been occupied for twenty years in amassing. He was not, it is true, so incredulous regarding the audacity of brigand behaviour as during the first twelve hours of his capture; but he did not believe that they would proceed to such extremities as those at which the brigand chief was wont to hint. When, as often happened, the camp was short of food, under which circumstances the prisoners' fare was neither better nor worse than that of their captors, the merchant was more depressed than in the days of plenty; but otherwise, and provided the night's march had been of moderate length—for they always migrated to some new spot as soon as the moon rose— he was cheerful, and inclined for talk with Walter. They had been now a week up in the mountains, without any news from Palermo, and during that period, besides repeating those favourite fragments of his autobiography respecting his early struggles with which his companion was already acquainted, he had become unexpectedly communicative with him concerning his domestic affairs. It was easy to see that Sir Reginald Selwyn, Baronet of the United Kingdom, was no longer an object of admiration with his father-in-law, and his antipathy towards him obviously increased with every day's delay in the arrival of the ransom. A man of business would have got the thing managed within twenty-four hours of the receipt of the authorization, he would say; and a man of courage and action, such as Sir Reginald had the reputation of being, would have seen that the troops had made short work of the brigands, and procured their release that way; but as it was, nothing was done, and there might just as well be no Sir Reginald in existence. Of course, it would have been easy for Walter to have inflamed the old merchant's mind against his relative still more, by merely relating the truth about him, but he did all he could to discourage the topic; yet he could not help learning some particulars of the voyage from England in the *Sylphide*, which certainly showed the ex-dragoon in no favourable light. In that limited sphere of existence, and always under the eye of his companions, Sir Reginald had not been quite so successful as at Willowbank in concealing his true character. His harshness to Lotty, which her sister's eyes had long detected, had become visible to her father's also, who had not hesitated to express his opinion on the subject; the baronet, too, in a moment of ungovernable ill-temper, had expressed his own, which

was to the effect that persons in business
had better stick to their business, for which
they alone were fitted, and not interfere
with officers and gentlemen in matters of
behaviour, of which they were not qualified
to judge. There had been in fact what
Mr. John Pelter would have designated
as "a rough-and-tumble" between the
old merchant and his son-in-law, and
though the quarrel had been patched up,
the sticking-plaster had evidently been
inefficient.

"I am not a man to be blinded by the
glitter of a title, Mr. Litton," said Mr.
Christopher Brown, "and you will remember how, from the very first, I opposed
myself to poor Lotty's marriage with this
gentleman. It would have been better for
my own peace of mind if I had been less
soft-hearted, and refused to countenance it
at all. It was wrong in me, as a matter of
principle, in my position as a father whose
wishes had been placed at defiance. The
money that that fellow has had out of me
in one way or another," added he, with an
irritation that took his would-be dignity off
its legs, "would astonish you, Mr. Litton;

and my impression is that that money has been thrown away."

So frankly, indeed, did Mr. Brown converse about his domestic relations and private affairs, that Walter, feeling it was only to the circumstances of their position that he owed this confidence, and that in case the merchant should regain his liberty he would repent of his candour, was quite embarrassed, and did all he could to turn the conversation into another channel. He questioned him about the time he had spent at Palermo—and, strangely enough, Mr. Brown never reciprocated this curiosity; either his egotism forbade him to inquire what had brought Walter to Sicily, or, having some suspicion of the cause, he refrained from alluding to it. Concerning the circumstances of his own capture, however, the merchant conversed readily enough. He was always, indeed, eager for talk— perhaps because it prevented him from indulging in melancholy reflections, or apprehensions which were more serious than he cared to own. The seizure of the *Sylphide* had happened almost as much by accident as design, or rather luck had be-

friended the brigands to an extraordinary
degree. Had even the light wind held
with which the yacht had sailed from
Palermo, its owner would have escaped
their hands; but they had speculated upon
the very thing that had taken place, and
been successful. Unwilling to lose so great
a prize as the person of the English Milord,
the hope of which had animated them for
weeks, they had followed the course of his
vessel, which was of necessity along the
coast and close in shore; and, under cover
of the night, embarking in a small fishing-
boat, had boarded her in sufficient numbers
to make resistance from unarmed men,
taken unawares, without avail. The steers-
man, who was the only one on deck at the
time of the seizure, had indeed tried to give
the alarm, for which he had paid the
penalty with his life's blood—the traces of
which Walter and Francisco had discovered;
but the rest of the crew had been over-
powered without a struggle, and since it
was by no means Corralli's policy to en-
cumber himself with useless prisoners, had
been set upon the road to Messina, from
which far-away town no danger could be

apprehended from the troops for many days. Lest any of these sailors should make their way back to Palermo, the road, as we have seen, had been strictly guarded, though that of course did not prevent Francisco's return to that city, upon whose report no doubt the soldiers had been sent out by the governor.

It was to the well-meant efforts of these emissaries of justice that the inconveniences of Mr. Brown and Walter were now owing, and to which it seemed only too likely that their lives would in the end be sacrificed. It was positively certain that Corralli would never permit his prestige to suffer by allowing them to be rescued alive out of his power; and, on the other hand, the cordon was drawn so strictly all around them, that it was most improbable that those in charge of the ransom would be able to break through, and reach their ever-shifting camp. It was not even certain—for they had had no news from the city since Lilian had been sent back—that the ransom was on its way. Poor Mr. Brown had now become as eager to pay it as he had previously been dis_inclined to do so; but the professional philosophy that caused him to regard it as a bad debt, had given way to more serious considerations. He had got to understand that it was very literally the price of his blood. Fatigue and privations had not only shaken his determination, but long experience of his lawless masters had somewhat opened his eyes to their true character, and to the perils of his own position. He perceived that his throat was likely to be cut at any moment before he could cry " Police !" and that it would be of no use to cry it, even if he should have time; but he did not understand yet that matters might take such a turn that he would be even glad to be put out of life by that summary process. Walter, however, from scraps of talk that he picked up from members of the band, was well aware that some terrible steps were in contemplation, in case the three hundred thousand ducats were not presently forthcoming. For one thing, both he and his companion had been carefully searched, and a penknife, which had been found upon Mr. Brown, had been taken from him—in order no doubt to prevent

his anticipating their cruel treatment, by
putting an end to his own existence. The
old merchant affected to attribute this to
mere malevolence, and bewailed the loss of
the little instrument, because of its business
associations—he had had it, he said, for
twenty years, and had never mended a pen
with any other blade; but it was doubtful
whether he himself had not some inkling
of the fate in preparation for him. As to
Corralli, he maintained a gloomy reserve,
never addressing himself to his captives, as
heretofore, but regarding them with a significant scowl, whenever his frowning eyes
chanced to fall upon them. They were
more strictly guarded too than ever, nor
were they permitted, as before, to be
together, but were located at opposite ends
of the camp. It seemed to Walter that he
had heard of some such arrangement being
made with respect to animals which were
destined for the butcher's knife. In their
case, it was not the way to fatten them, for,
deprived of his companion, the poor merchant began to lose health, and flesh, and
spirits; nor did his appetite, which he had

possessed at first in such vigour, remain to
him.   It must be confessed that there was
not much to tempt it.   The cordon drawn
by the soldiers grew every day more strict,
and made the task of provisioning the
brigands very difficult to the wretched
peasants who undertook it at the twofold
risk of their lives.   They were shot by the
military, if detected in aiding or abetting
the bandits ; and they were certain to fall
victims to the latter, when the troops should
withdraw, in case they omitted to provide
them with food.   It sometimes happened
that for days together no supplies could be
brought up, and then some of the band
would steal down the mountain, under
cover of the night, and bring back what
they could : hard cabbage and garlic plucked
from some village garden, a piece of sour
cheese, and as much black bread as they
could carry.   It was a feast-day when they
came upon a herd of sheep and goats—when
they got as much milk as they could drink,
and ate the mutton almost raw—with such
infinite precautions had the fire to be
kindled for cooking it, and of such small
dimensions was its flame.   And all this

time the captives had no change of linen,
and only on very rare occasions were they
permitted the use of water.

When they had been living for more than
a fortnight under these wretched conditions,
which, as Walter at least was well convinced,
were not likely to be exchanged for better
ones, an incident happened which for the
moment filled all hearts with joy. A little
after sunrise one morning the brigand call
was heard in the valley to westward—that
is, in the direction of Palermo—and the whole
camp was at once on the *qui vive.* Certain
members of the band had been stationed in
the neighbourhood of the city, to expedite
the arrival of the ransom, and it was con-
fidently expected that they had now arrived
with their precious burden. Even Corralli's
face expanded into a grim smile at the prospect of this happy result, and for the first
time for days he addressed a few words to
Walter.

"It is very well both for you and for me,"
said he, "that I have been so long-suffering;
but, to say the truth, my patience had
almost reached the end of her tether."

To Mr. Brown he even now did not deign

to speak, but regarded him with a grudging look, as a victim who had escaped his vengeance, and whom he regretted to see depart with a whole skin. As for the rest of the band, they had no such repinings; some evinced a childish delight by leaping and dancing, and others already began to gamble in anticipation of the gold that was presently to fill their pockets. In the meantime, Canelli had been sent down to see that all was right, and welcome the newcomers. Presently he reappeared, making the signal of "no danger," but not that which had been agreed upon to signify the arrival of the treasure. The captives were not aware of the reason, but they saw that Corralli's face began to gloom, and a shadow had fallen on the general gaiety.

Following Canelli were now seen two striplings, looking even younger than himself.

"They can surely never have entrusted so much money to boys like that," observed Mr. Brown, who had begun to feel uneasy.

"Alas!" said Walter, "I fear there is no money."

"Then Heaven help us," sighed the

merchant despairingly, "for I believe that man will shed our blood."

Walter did not answer; he had recognised Joanna and Lavocca in the two newcomers, and a gleam of hope shot into his heart. He felt confident that the former would help them if she could.

The two women came up the hill without raising their eyes from the ground, and Canelli, as he drew nigh, kept shaking his head. It was easy to see that they had brought neither ransom nor good news.

"What brings you here, Joanna," inquired the brigand chief, in displeased tones, "when I bade you stay in the cave until you heard from me?"

"A very ugly reason—the mere want of meat and drink, brother," answered she, with an attempt at lightness in her tone. "The villagers have brought us nothing for these three days, on account of the soldiers."

Joanna's swarthy face was very pale, and her large eyes seemed to stand out from her sunken cheeks. Lavocca looked in even worse case, and when she had with difficulty reached the first tree that fringed their camp she held on to it, as though her limbs needed support. It was evident that both of them were half-starved. Santoro was bounding forward to welcome his sweetheart, when the captain grasped his arm, and pushed him back. "Look to your prisoner," cried he gruffly; "that is your first duty. Corbara, let the women have food."

It was an order by no means easy to execute, yet some morsels of coarse bread were handed to them, and a few drops of wine in a tin cup.

When they had refreshed themselves, Corralli began to make a speech, to which every one listened with the utmost interest. His words were uttered with such haste and passion, that Walter could with difficulty catch his meaning; but he seemed to be narrating the history of the band during the last few weeks. Whenever he alluded to his prisoners his tone increased in bitterness, and he pointed rapidly from one to the other, and then in the direction of Palermo. The words "starvation," "loss," and "death" recurred again and again, and then he drew attention to the wasted forms and

pale faces of the women. It was plain that
he was crediting the unhappy captives with
all the misfortunes that had befallen them
since the soldiers had been called out.
"And this ransom," continued he, speaking
more slowly, and casting an inquiring look
around the band—"this ransom that was to
pay us for all our trouble, and which we
thought had just come to hand, where is it?
Have we heard even if it exists, or if the
bankers are willing to pay it? No; we
have heard nothing."

"Nothing — nothing!" echoed the
brigands gloomily.

"For all we know, this old man here
may have been aware from the first that the
money would not be sent; there may have
been something wrong—purposely wrong—
in his letter of authorization ; he may have
trusted all along to the chapter of accidents,
to the chances of escape, or of his being
rescued by the troops; and, in the meantime, he may have been making fools of
us."

A menacing murmur broke out at this,
and many a face was turned with fury in
the direction of the unhappy merchant,

who, pale and trembling with apprehensions of he knew not what, looked eagerly at Walter, as though he had not been as powerless as himself.

"At all events," resumed the chief, after a judicious pause, "it is my opinion that it would be idle to wait this gentleman's pleasure any longer. As it is, we have borne with him far more patiently than is customary with us, and folks are beginning to say—'This Corralli and his men are not what they were; the presence of the soldiers alarms them; captives have only to be obstinate enough, and they will carry their point against these stupid brigands.'"

"Stupid?" repeated Corbara, playing with his knife, and glaring from Walter to Mr. Brown, as though debating with himself upon which to commence his operations. "We will let them know that we are not stupid."

"It has always hitherto been our rule, that when a ransom is not settled within a reasonable time, the captive should pay it in another fashion," proceeded Corralli; "and in this case, when we have been driven from our camping-ground, shot at

by the troops, into whose hands two of our
men have fallen, and by whom one has
been slain, is it right that we should make
an exception ? Shall we ever see Manfred
again, or Duano, think you?"

" Never !" cried the brigands gloomily ;
" they are as good as dead."

" We have the absence therefore of
three friends to avenge ; one life, as it were,
to count against us in any case. These
two should therefore not be permitted to
die slowly."

" You are right, captain," said Corbara,
drawing his hand across his mouth, which
always watered at the prospect of a wickedness. " But there is no reason why we
should not set about the matter at once."

The two brigands to whose custody Mr.
Brown was confided here each laid a hand
upon his wrist, and Santoro and Colletta
drew a pace nearer to Walter. It was
evident that the long-delayed hour of
revenge had come at last.

" I would wish to say a word or two,
brother," said a soft, clear voice, " before a
deed is done of which we may all repent
ourselves."

"You may say what you please, Joanna," observed Corralli coldly; "these men, however, are not your prisoners, but ours."

"The English girl was mine, until you sent me word that she was to be set free," answered Joanna coldly; "and since you have taken her, I claim him yonder"—and she pointed to Walter—"as my captive in her place."

A shout of disapprobation burst from all sides at this audacious demand.

"It seems to me that the signora has fallen in love with our young Englishman," laughed Corbara coarsely.

Joanna's eyes flashed fire, and her cheek lost all its paleness for an instant, as the words met her ear; but she answered nothing, only looked with passionate appeal towards her brother, as though she would have said: "It is your place to cut that fellow's tongue out."

"Indeed, Joanna," answered he coldly, "such a proposal as yours seems to me to excuse a man's saying almost anything. These Englishmen are the common property of us all, and though it is true the signora was

given to yourself, yet she was set free with a
view to benefit you. You would have had a
fair share of the ransom, had it been obtained,
but it has not been obtained, and it is no
fault of ours that the retaliation we intend
to take for its non-arrival will not afford you
gratification."

" Gratification !" echoed she contemptuously. " When these men are dead
—to-morrow, or the next day, or even the
day after—will the recollection of your
cruelties be worth to you three hundred
thousand ducats ? That the money has
not arrived is not their fault, but yours. If
you had sent some responsible person to
manage the affair, instead of a dying
woman, you would have all been rich men
by this time. Why, for all you know, she
may never have reached the city alive,
much more in a condition to settle matters
with the bankers. Ask Santoro there,
who helped to take her down to the
village, whether she looked more dead or
alive."

" The signora was very weak and ill, no
doubt," said Santoro, upon whom a pleading
look from Lavocca had not been thrown

away. "It was my belief that she would not get over the journey."

"And yet you entrusted this important affair to such an envoy!" continued Joanna bitterly. "One would think that three hundred thousand ducats was a sum as easily extracted as the ransom of a village mayor."

"It is doubtless a large sum," observed Corralli coldly; "and since it has not been paid, the forfeit will be made proportionate."

"Yes; but it would have been paid had you gone the right way about it; and if you are not all mad, or thirsting for blood, like that brute Corbara yonder, you may have it yet. Think, my friends, of what may be purchased for three hundred thousand ducats, and how much greater pleasure you will take in the spending of it than in what you now propose to do!"

"What you say is doubtless very true, Joanna," replied Corralli in the same tone; "but unless you have something else to propose to us than to have patience——"

"I *have* something else to propose,"

interrupted she ; " I suggest that the error which you committed in sending a dying woman to negotiate so important an affair shall be repaired. Let another envoy be chosen, who will not let the grass grow under his feet. You talk of precedents, and surely this has often been done before. When a captive is taken with a servant, is it not our custom to send home the man to manage matters for his master's release? And though it is true this young Englishman here is no servant, he is of no more value to us in the way of ransom than if he were ; while, on the other hand, he understands Milord's affairs far better, being his friend."

" It seems to me, captain, that there really is something in this," observed Santoro, on whom the masked battery of Lavocca's eyes had been playing incessantly during her mistress's speech.

" Something, yes," laughed Corbara scornfully ; " and it is easy enough to see what it is, so far as the signora is concerned."

Corralli looked carelessly about him, as though to invite others to express their opinions, if they were so pleased, and presently his eye fell on Canelli.'

"Come, you are the youngest of us," said he, "and are not prejudiced in favour of brigand customs. How does it strike you, merely judging by common sense, with respect to this proposition of my sister's?"

"Indeed, it seems to me," returned the lad, with a glance of ill-favour towards Walter, "that a bird in the hand is always worth two in the bush."

"Or rather, you should say in this case, Canelli, that two birds in the hand are worth one in the bush," observed the captain; a sally which evoked approbation, but no laughter, a sign that the brigands' humour was serious indeed. "You see, my dear Joanna," continued Corralli gravely, "that the opinion of us all—or nearly all—is opposed to yours in the matter; and, for my part, I do not wonder at it. It is true that this gentleman"—here he pointed to Walter—"is poor; but we fixed his ransom at a certain insignificant sum — three thousand ducats—which has not been paid. His life therefore is forfeited as much as Milord's yonder. If we send him on this embassy, what guarantee should we have that we shall ever see him again? At present we have his skin; but if he gets to Palermo, he will pay us neither in purse nor person."

"That is as clear as the sunshine," observed Canelli approvingly; "there will be but one prisoner left to us out of three, and not a single ducat."

"That is so," murmured a dozen voices. Even Santoro was obliged to acknowledge the merciless correctness of this arithmetic.

"You shall not lose the ducats," answered Joanna steadily. "In case the young man does not return on the appointed day, I will pay his ransom out of my own purse."

"You must be mad, Joanna," cried Corralli angrily.

"On the contrary, it is you that are mad, Rocco, who will risk nothing when there is a prospect of gaining so much. I see plainly that by this plan we shall gain all we have looked for, and I am not blinded by passion, like some of you."

"By Heaven, I am not sure of that!" muttered Corralli between his teeth.

"At all events, my friends, you will have

the three thousand ducats to do what you please with," said Joanna; "and if one of you should win it all at baccara, he will have a fortune."

"I like that idea, I confess," observed Colletta, who had great luck at cards; "besides, we should still have Milord yonder to amuse us;" and he pointed to the unhappy merchant, who, having long given up the attempt to understand what was going on, had sat himself down cross-legged, more melancholy than any tailor in a "sweater's" shop.

"In order that there may be no doubt about the matter, my friends," said Joanna, "you shall have the three thousand ducats at once—Santoro yonder knows where they are kept, and shall go with any one of you to fetch them this very moment."

Eloquence and logic are both very well in their way, but the conviction they carry with them is light when compared with the persuasive power of ready money. The captain indeed was displeased, not so much that Walter should escape him, as because he felt that Joanna had made a fool of herself on account of the young fellow, and

that the three thousand ducats would be a
dead "loss to the family;" and Corbara was
furious, since the cruelties for which he had
as morbid an appetite as an American
Indian, must necessarily be delayed. But,
with these exceptions, the whole band were
now in favour of Joanna's plan.

Walter had listened to these proceedings
with intense interest, but even when the
moment had apparently arrived for his being
put to the most cruel tortures, he had
scarcely been more moved than when he
heard the generous proposal of his late
hostess. While it was in debate he had
uttered not a syllable, nor even by a look
expressed the gratitude with which it had
inspired him, lest he should do it prejudice;
but now that matters had declared themselves in his favour, he addressed the
brigand chief as follows : "I am fully aware,
Captain Corralli, of the great kindness
which your sister has shown me, and of the
generosity of the offer she has made ; it is
impossible for me to overrate the confidence
she has reposed in me ; but you may be
certain of this, that it is not misplaced. If
I am alive, I shall return to you at any

reasonable date you may please to fix, either with my ransom or without it."

"And with your friend the Milord's ransom," put in the captain quickly. "It is on that account—and not upon your own, remember—that we give you permission to depart."

Joanna was about to speak, but Corralli stopped her angrily: "You have got your way, woman, and be content with it. The arrangement of the rest of the affair remains in my hands. To-day is Tuesday. You will understand, then, at this hour, at eight o'clock in the morning"—and the captain again indulged himself in consulting one of his splendid watches—"you will present yourself on this very spot on Friday."

"The time is very short," pleaded Walter, "since there may be much to be done."

"Then we will say eight o'clock in the evening, which will give you twelve hours more. At eight o'clock next Friday evening, then, we shall know whether an Englishman can be trusted to keep his word or not. After that hour, we shall begin to send you little mementoes of your fellow-countryman yonder; first his ears, next his fingers, and then one by one his larger limbs, till he becomes a torso. If the word of an Englishman should fail, that of a Sicilian will not ; I mean it, by Santa Rosalia !" And the captain took a silver image of the local saint that hung about his neck, and kissed it fervently, as an honest witness does the Testament at the Old Bailey.

" O Walter, Walter, you are not going to leave me !" cried the old merchant wofully, perceiving that his friend was about to depart.

" I shall come back again, Mr. Brown ; I shall indeed."

" No, no ; you will never do that," exclaimed the other despairingly ; "it is contrary to human nature."

" I will, sir. So Heaven help me ! as I am a Christian man, and a gentleman, I will return, either to set you free, or to die with you. There is some hitch about the ransom, and I am going to Palermo to expedite matters. Don't fret, sir ; all will be well yet, thanks to this generous lady."

Poor Mr. Brown's sagacity had by no means penetrated the disguises of Joanna and Lavocca ; if he had done so, and had

understood the nature of the obligation
which the former had conferred upon him,
he would doubtless have duly acknowledged
it; as it was he only looked wildly round
in search of a female form. Walter, who
had been permitted to cross the camp to bid
his friend farewell, explained to him, not
without some embarrassment, how matters
stood.

"But what has made the woman so civil
to us?" inquired the merchant eagerly.

"She has a kind heart; it was she who
sent the bread and mutton, when you were
half-starved the other day."

"But she has got pistols in her sash, and
a long knife," expostulated Mr. Brown,
"and she wears——"

"Hush! yes; never mind. I must go
now, for every minute is precious. Is it
possible, think you, that anything should be
added to the authorization you sent by
Lilian?"

"Nothing; it was quite in form. Still I
will write one line, if these wretches will
give me pen and paper."

Corralli produced the necessary implements, and the merchant wrote: "Spare no

expense, and trust implicitly the bearer; (signed) CHRISTOPHER BROWN." Give my dear love to Lilian, and should I never see her again, nor you——"

"You will see me again this day week," interrupted Walter hastily; he thought it base to take advantage of such an opportunity, though it was evident that the merchant had been about to couple his name with Lilian's. "Good-bye, sir, for the present, and be of good courage."

" Farewell, Walter, farewell; and God be with you!" answered the old man, with choking voice.

" Amen!" replied Walter solemnly.

Then the members of the band, with the exception of Corbara, who stood scowling apart, flocked round him to bid him good-bye; the same hands which had been itching to inflict death and torture upon him an hour ago being now held forth to him with good-will, and even gaiety. Corralli alone was grave.

"You will not misunderstand your countryman's position here, because of all this," said he, alluding to these manifestations of friendship.

"Neither his, nor my own," answered Walter with dignity. "I know there is no mercy to be expected for either of us, in case the ransom is not forthcoming."

"And yet you will keep your word?"

"And yet I shall keep my word."

The captain smiled incredulously as he held out his hand. "Santoro here will be your guide to Palermo—and back again, if you ever do come back."

Then Walter looked about him for Joanna, for whose ear he had reserved some heartfelt expressions of gratitude; but both she and Lavocca had disappeared. He was distressed at this, yet at the same time was conscious of a sense of intense relief. He felt that Corbara had been right in imputing to the chief's sister a personal affection for himself, which it was impossible he could reciprocate. In that supreme moment all coxcombry was out of the question, and matters were compelled to present themselves in their true light. Joanna loved him; and since he loved another, it almost seemed to him, though guiltless of deceit, that he had obtained the precious boon of freedom under false pretences.

CHAPTER VI.

SIR REGINALD TAKES HIS OWN VIEW.

S Walter descended the mountain, accompanied by Santoro, his reflections did not permit him to pay much attention to the incidents of the way: when they had to let themselves down some precipice, his foot and hand indeed obeyed his will; and when, now and then, his companion bade him listen, in fear that they were approaching the troops, who would certainly have shot them both, without waiting for an explanation, he stopped and listened mechanically; but for the most part his own thoughts preoccupied him, and he only knew, or cared to know, that the direction in which he was advancing with such rapid strides was towards Palermo. The sense of sudden freedom did not occur

to him with the force it had done when
standing with Joanna in front of the cavern;
for he was even less free now than he had
been then; but the question, whether he
should have his freedom eventually, agitated
his mind perpetually.   How many of us, in
supreme moments—those of dangerous illness of ourselves or of others; or when
prosperity or poverty is trembling in the
balance; or when we await Yes or No
from lips we love—have said to ourselves:
" How will it be with me to-morrow; or the
next hour; or when I shall presently return
out of that door?"   And so it was with
Walter, as, free of limb, but a slave to his
plighted word, he descended that Sicilian
hill-side.   " How will it be with me four
days hence, when I shall have to return
yonder, laden with the gold that will be the
price of our freedom, or empty-handed, and
therefore doomed to death amid unspeakable
torments?"   Nor was it egotism—though
egotism would, under such circumstances,
have been very pardonable—that moved the
young man to these considerations.   Life
was dear to him no doubt, as it is dear to
most of us at five-and-twenty, but there

were dearer things than life concerned with
that alternative which he was considering.
If, for example, he should not obtain the
ransom, the cause of his failure would in all
probability be what Joanna had suggested
—namely, the inability of Lilian to prosecute
the matter. She might have been too ill
even to speak of it, or to place the authorization in Sir Reginald's hands, on her arrival
in Palermo; she might be delirious, and up
to this hour have remembered nothing of
the charge confided to her; or she might
be dead. A cold stone seemed to take the
place of Walter's heart as this last idea
occurred to him. If she was dead, what
mattered it how it should be with him next
week, or any week! He would die too, and
thereby avoid breaking his word, for he had
said: " I will return if I am alive." No;
that would be only keeping his promise to
the ear: he must live on, for the sake of the
poor old man he had just left among those
merciless wretches; must do his best for his
enfranchisement, or comfort him by his
presence in his miserable fate; for would
not Lilian have had it so!

"Stop, signor; there go the soldiers,"

said Santoro; and on the road which had last come into view before them could be seen through the trees a considerable body of troops moving towards the city.

"The cordon must be loosening," observed Santoro, "unless these men have been relieved. Now is the time to get money up to the camp, if we could only know where it was."

This was clear enough, and Walter was for pushing on at increased speed; but Santoro bade him pause, lest there should be more soldiers returning home, and they should find themselves between two detachments. The wisdom of this advice was made evident within the next quarter of an hour by the appearance of another body of men almost as large as that which had preceded it.

"The troops have been recalled," murmured Santoro triumphantly. "The governor has grown tired of hunting us with the troops, and the road for the ransom is now clear."

"Let us hope so," answered Walter fervently; "but is it not possible that they have intercepted it?"

It was not unusual in similar cases for the Government to direct the division of the money among the troops ; for though it made feeble efforts to put down the brigands, it was high-handed enough in its measures respecting the illegal payment of the ransoms of their victims.

" No, no ; the soldiers would have talked and sung as they went by, had they had any success. Take my word for it, they have given up the whole thing, and have gone home in disgust."

At all events Walter and his companion met with no further hindrance, and reached Palermo before dusk. Santoro, it was agreed, should not enter the city in his company, lest his connexion with the brigands—though having divested himself of his arms and jewels he looked as " indifferent honest" as any other of his fellow-countrymen—should be taken for granted ; and the gate of the English burial-ground having been fixed upon as a place of rendezvous every evening, in case they should wish to communicate with one another, for the present they parted ; Santoro, in the highest spirits at the pro-

spect of a few days of town-life, directing
his steps to some friends in the neighbourhood of the Dogana, and Walter to the
hotel upon the Marina at which Sir
Reginald had lodged, and to which he did
not doubt that Lilian would have been
carried. He had some hesitation as to
whether he should ask to see her or the
baronet; but on consideration of the importance of the matter at stake, which seemed
to override all ordinary and conventional
rules, he determined on presenting himself
to Lilian. But in the first place it was
absolutely necessary that he should seek
his own lodgings on the Marina. Unshaven,
unwashed, ragged, and scorched with the
sun, he looked more like a native beggar
than the young English gentleman who had
embarked in pursuit of the *Sylphide* some
fifteen days ago. Baccari, who was standing at his house door, did not even move
aside as he approached, but regarded him
with no very favourable expression.

"I have nothing for you, nor such as
you," said he, anticipating from this able-
bodied but dilapidated stranger an application for alms.

" What! Baccari, has a fortnight's stay
with Captain Corralli then so altered your
old lodger?"

In a moment the honest little fellow had
thrown himself about Walter's neck, and
was weeping tears of joy.

." Thanks be to Heaven and all the
saints," cried he, "that you have returned
alive! Come in, come in! What a spectacle do I behold! Nothing has happened
like it since my neighbour Loffredo's case.
O the villains, the scoundrels! Welcome
home! A bath? Of course you desire a
bath. I recognise you for an Englishman
by that request, though otherwise you
might be a countryman of my own—and by
Santa Rosalia, not one of the most respectable. You must be half-starved, my
dear young sir; still you are alive and have
come back again from that den of thieves.
How delighted Francisco will be! The
poor youth has never been himself since
you left him, in spite of his good advice,
and fell into the hands of those ruffians.
Signor Pelter too, I shall not now have to
write to him to say: 'Our friend has been
put to death by brigands.'" While

supplying his guest with food and everything needful, the good lodging-house
keeper did not in fact for a moment cease
expressing his thanks to Providence and
his congratulations on Walter's safe return.
For the time such genuine manifestations
of good-will, succeeding to such hard conditions of life as those to which he had been
of late accustomed, quite won the young
painter from his despondency, and almost
convinced him that he had really regained
home and safety. But no sooner had he
recruited his strength and attired himself in
a decent garb, than the responsibilities of
his mission began to press upon him.
Indeed, more than once had an inquiry
concerning Lilian been upon his lips, which
nevertheless he had not the courage to
frame. At last he turned round boldly to
his host. "And now," said he, " tell me
about the English lady whom Corralli
caused to be sent back to Palermo. Since
her father is still in his hands, I am come
hither to effect the payment of his ransom."

"Ah! the ransom. Well, yesterday I
should have said you would have had but a
bad chance, even supposing, as I do not

doubt, that you have the means of raising the money. The governor, you see, is very indignant at the outrage, since it has happened to a rich Englishman, and not to a poor devil of a fellow-countryman like myself. Sir Reginald, too, and the British consul have been very importunate with him. Half the troops in the city have therefore been sent out to hunt the brigands, with strict orders also, you may be sure, to let no money-bags pass through their lines. But to-day, as I hear, the soldiers have been recalled, since Corralli and his men have taken their departure towards Messina."

"But the young lady—Mr. Brown's daughter—you tell me nothing of her."

"Well, indeed, my dear young sir, there is but little to tell; no one has seen her since she was brought home to the hotel yonder, more dead than alive, except her sister and Julia?"

"Who is Julia?"

"Oh! that is the waiting-maid whose services have been secured for her, and about whom my son Francisco will tell you a great deal more than I can. I am very much afraid that the boy will marry her,

and then there will be a family to keep by
fishing, I suppose, and the little I can afford
to contribute. They will want the house
too for the children, and I shall be no
longer enabled to let lodgings."

"For Heaven's sake, tell me about the
young lady! Is she worse or better? Is
she in danger?"

"I don't know about danger, but she is
still very ill, I believe, and unfortunately
wandering in her mind. The sun, it seems,
was too much for her during that noontide
journey, and she was ill before. My good
sir, where are you going? It is out of the
question that she should be able to see you."

"Then I must see Sir Reginald," said
Walter decisively; "it is upon a matter
that does not admit of a moment's delay."
Upon the whole, he thought it wise not to
communicate to the talkative Sicilian what
the matter really was; if the authorities
had really opposed themselves to the money
being paid, the more secretly the affair was
managed the better.

"Well, if it is about Milord's freedom
and the ransom," observed Baccari with an
aggrieved air, "you may consider that as a

public topic. Every one is talking about it: some say one thing indeed, and some another, but I can tell you this much—who have, unfortunately, had some experience in these matters—that hitherto Sir Reginald and the rest of them have been going the wrong way to work to procure your countryman's freedom; and not only the wrong way, but the very way to prevent it. Let the gold be put in a box—the money must be paid in gold, of course—and let it be carried out at night up to Corralli's camp; then Milord will come down in the morning, a little thinner perhaps, and by no means pleased with our Sicilian ways (none of Corralli's captives are): but, after all, there will have been no harm done. Whereas, to send troops after these gentry is the way to make them flit—flit like cloud-shadows, from hill-side to hill-side, and take their prisoner with them, until one day they get tired of carrying him about, and cut his throat."

" That is precisely my own view of the matter," answered Walter thoughtfully.

" Just so; and you have had a personal experience. Up to this moment, you will

bear me witness, my dear young sir, that I
have not put one question to you; though
I have been hungering to learn your adven-
tures almost as much as you were for your
dinner. How did you fare? How did you
sleep? Were there more than fifty of those
scoundrels? (for that is what is reported).
Did you see Joanna, who is dressed as a
man?"

" My dear Baccari, I will tell you all that
another time, but for the present I have
not a moment at my own disposal."

And Walter took up his hat, and turned
his steps to the hotel, which was but a few
paces off. The brief exhilaration caused by
good food and clean raiment—and by the
latter scarcely less than the former—had
now passed away, and his mind was full of
forebodings. If he should be really unable
to gain speech with Lilian, it would be
difficult, he knew, to persuade Sir Reginald
to change any course of action which he had
once seen proper to adopt—difficult under
any conditions; but now that they had
ceased to be friends—not to say had become
enemies—it was a task of which he well-
nigh despaired. It was true there were

other strings to his bow—the bankers, the
consul, to be applied to, with whom surely
his late experience, and the conviction that
was born of it, must needs have some weight.
But even his own impressions—notwithstanding that he felt himself as much tied
and bound by his promise to the brigand
chief as ever—were far different, now that
he was free and among friends, than what
they had been when in captivity; and he
was well aware that it would not be easy to
convince men who were living at home at
ease of the desperate condition in which
himself and the old merchant really stood.
On arriving at the hotel therefore, notwithstanding that such a proceeding might of
itself enrage Sir Reginald against him, he
asked to see Miss Lilian Brown.   The
porter, however, accustomed to continual
inquiries upon the part of the British residents after her health, misunderstood his
words, and replied that the young lady's
condition was slightly improving, but that
she had not yet recovered her senses.   This
was as bad as anything Walter could have
expected, and of course put a stop to any
idea of a personal interview.

"I wish to see her brother-in-law, Sir Reginald Selwyn," observed he, "upon business of great importance."

"Very good, sir. This way, if you please."

As Walter followed the man upstairs, the terrible thought invaded his mind that perhaps this poor girl had not been in her right mind since her arrival; that nothing had been done with respect to the authorization, and that everything connected with the ransom would have to begin *de novo.* If the bankers in Palermo were as dilatory as the rest of their fellow-countrymen in matters of business, the time before him was short indeed. Walter was ushered into a sitting-room upon the first-floor, and requested to wait while his name was sent up to the baronet.

"It is unnecessary to give my name," said he, after a moment's reflection; "you may say an old acquaintance from England."

It was just possible, he thought, that Sir Reginald might decline to see his quondam friend, after what had happened at their last meeting at Willowbank; and, moreover, he wished to judge from the baronet's countenance whether his presence in Palermo took him by surprise or not; since, if it did, it would be proof that Lilian had never been in a condition to relate to him what had taken place during her captivity. It was nearly a quarter of an hour before Sir Reginald made his appearance, expecting doubtless to see some casual London acquaintance, who, finding him at Palermo, had dropped in for an evening call.

His countenance changed directly he set eyes on Walter; he did not, however, seem so much surprised as annoyed and disappointed: his look of conventional welcome at once gave place to one of dislike and suspicion.

"This is an unexpected pleasure, Mr. Litton," said he coldly, and pointing to a chair.

Walter sat down. Such a reception was almost an insult, but the circumstances were too serious to admit of his taking offence.

"You knew I was in Palermo, Sir Reginald, or at least that I had been so, I conclude?"

The baronet hesitated: "Yes; I have heard so."

"And also that I had been taken prisoner by the brigands, in company with your father-in-law, who is still unhappily in their hands?"

"I did not hear that you were in his company when taken prisoner; indeed, I had reason to suppose that such would hardly have been the case."

This allusion to the merchant's quarrel with Walter, fomented as it had been by the speaker himself, and indeed solely attributable to him, was almost too much for Walter's patience; still he kept his temper.

"I was made captive, Sir Reginald, as you say, not in Mr. Brown's company, but in the attempt to give the alarm while there was yet time; I hoped to effect his release by force of arms. That time is unfortunately past; and it is my painful duty to inform you, that if immediate steps are not taken to pay his ransom, his life will without doubt be forfeited."

"That is what Captain Corralli says, I suppose," observed Sir Reginald contemptuously.

" He has said so, and in such a matter he will, without doubt, keep his word. If within four days the whole three hundred thousand ducats are not in his hands——"

" Why, that is fifty thousand pounds!" interrupted Sir Reginald ; "a modest sum, truly, to be asked for by a highwayman."

" But is it possible that I am telling you this for the first time?" exclaimed Walter, feeling that his worst fears were indeed realized. " Did not Miss Lilian tell you with what mission she was charged?"

" My sister-in-law was brought to the city in a dangerous and almost desperate condition, quite unfit to attend to any matters of business."

" Business! But this is an affair that concerns her father's life. Do you mean to tell me that she never gave you the authorization for the payment of the money, which I saw Mr. Brown write out with his own hand ?"

" I have seen no such document, nor is any such in Miss Brown's possession," answered the baronet steadily. " As to the enormous sum you have mentioned, it is true that she has spoken of it more than once, but it was very naturally taken as the utterance of a disordered intellect. She has been wandering in her mind—as well as prostrated by fever—ever since her return."

"The sum is perfectly correct, Sir Reginald, and not a ducat less will be taken by the brigand chief. It is the price of Mr. Brown's life—and of my life also (though I do not wish to speak of that), since I have promised to return either with or without it within four days. We are both dead men if——"

"Excuse me, Mr. Litton," said Sir Reginald, smiling, "if I recommend that you should take some rest and refreshment before you speak any more on the topic. It evidently excites you, and if, as I conclude, you have just escaped from these scoundrels' hands, you are hardly fit to judge of them dispassionately. You are naturally disposed to exaggerate their power and determination, and to give them—or rather to persuade others to give them—whatever they choose to ask."

"Sir Reginald, I am as cool and collected as yourself; I have told you nothing which is not true, except that it is not the whole truth. Your father-in-law will be put to death—of that I am satisfied—in some most cruel and shocking fashion, if you turn a deaf ear to what I say. Ask any one in Palermo who is acquainted with the brigand customs in such cases, and I am confident they will bear me out in what I say."

"I scarcely think you are quite aware of *what* you say, Mr. Litton," answered the other, in a cold, calm voice: "you just expressed your resolve to return in person to these gentry, in order that you yourself may be put to death. You are a little eccentric in your conduct (if you will permit me to say so) even now, but you would, in that case, be stark staring mad."

"I know that many people think it madness to keep their word, when it happens to be to their disadvantage," answered Walter quietly; "but that is beside the question. I am pleading for your father-in-law, not for myself. And I must insist, in his name, and for his life's sake, that an immediate search be made for the authorization of which I have spoken."

There was a short pause, during which the baronet frowned heavily and bit his lip, as though in doubt. "The word 'insist' is one which is utterly out of place in this discussion," observed he presently; "but I make allowance for your excited condition, which indeed the circumstances of the case may well excuse. Moreover, I should be loth, for old acquaintance' sake, to refuse you satisfaction in so simple a matter." Here he rang the bell, and bade the servant request the presence of Lady Selwyn. "My wife," said he, "who is in constant attendance on her sister, shall at once make search for the paper of which you speak. I conclude you will trust to her report, if not to mine."

"Trust, Sir Reginald!" echoed Walter excitedly. "Do you suppose, then, that I think you capable of having ignored this authorization, or of concealing it? Why, if you knew of it, and yet kept it back, you would be a murderer—ay, just as much the assassin of your wife's father——"

"Here is my wife," broke in Sir Reginald. "Pray keep this extravagant talk of yours, Mr. Litton, somewhat within bounds, or at least reserve it for male ears." He spoke with sharpness as well as scorn, but Walter heeded him not; his whole attention was riveted by the appearance of Lotty, who was standing pale and trembling at the open door. She had evidently heard his words, and was looking at her husband with in- quiring yet frightened eyes. "A murderer!" she murmured—"an assassin!"

"Yes; those were the words this gentle- man used, and which he applied to me, madam," said the baronet scornfully. "Does it appear to you that I look like one or the other?"

"But what does he mean, Reginald?"

"Gad, madam, that is more than I can tell you. He has been raving here these twenty minutes about his friends the brigands, who have sent him, it seems, for a trifle of fifty thousand pounds, as the price of your father's release."

"As the price of his life, Lady Selwyn!" answered Walter solemnly. "He wrote out an order on the bankers for that sum, and sent it by your sister's hand; but Sir Reginald tells me it has not been found. I adjure you, if your father's existence is dear to you, to discover what has become of it."

"Indeed, Mr. Litton, I will do my best,"

said Lotty, with a glance at her husband, such as those animals who have been trained to do things contrary to their nature always throw at their master before commencing a performance. " My sister is very ill——"

" He knows all that," interrupted Sir Reginald hastily. "She is much too ill, of course, to be interrogated on any such matter. But, if the authorization—this document Mr. Litton speaks of—was confided to Lilian, it must of course be still in her possession. I don't say that I would act upon it, mind, even if it was found, sir," added he, as his wife left the room ; " my idea is, that one should never treat with these scoundrels save sword in hand; that we should give them lead and steel—not gold."

" Nay, Sir Reginald ; I am sure if you were to read your father-in-law's words, written as they were in the dire expectation of death, these scruples would weigh as nothing."

" Well, well, we shall see. I need not trouble you to wait ; but in case of Lady Selwyn's finding this document, I will send

word of the fact to your address, if you will
furnish me with it."

Sir Reginald took out his tablets, and
wrote down the number of Mr. Baccari's
house, like any other trifling memorandum.

His coolness seemed frightful to Walter.

"And if the document is *not* found, Sir
Reginald?"

"Well, really, in that case, I cannot see
what is to be done, more than has been
already done. The troops were promptly
sent out, and in considerable force——"

"They would have been useless in any
case," put in Walter earnestly; "but, as it
happens, they have been withdrawn——"

"Indeed! I had not heard of that,"
returned the other quickly.

"It matters not. I repeat, that all
armed intervention would be useless."

"You must really allow others as well
as yourself, Mr. Litton, to exercise some
judgment in this affair. The British
consul, the governor of the town, and the
humble individual who has the honour to
address you, are all of one opinion, and it is
diametrically opposed to your own. As to
the other matter, you shall be communi·

cated with, if the necessity arises. Good
morning to you."

Walter rose, and left the room without a
word. He could not trust himself to speak
more with this man, who treated the
capture and death of a fellow-creature—not
to mention that he was a near connexion
of his own—with such philosophic indifference. He could not imagine that he had
utterly failed to convince Sir Reginald of
the peril of his father-in-law's position.
On the contrary, a dreadful suspicion had
taken possession of him, that the baronet
was well aware of it, and had his own
reasons for affecting to ignore it. Why
should it have entered into his mind that
he (Walter) would not believe his report
concerning the existence of the authorization, unless he had been conscious of a wish
—perhaps an intention—that it should not
be found? If Lilian, who was said to be
seriously ill, were to die, the whole of her
father's wealth, should he be put to death
by the brigands, would revert to Sir Reginald, through Lotty. The perspiration
stood upon Walter's brow at the contemplation of such wickedness as these ideas sug-

gested, but yet they remained with him;
he did not, as of old, repent of having
entertained such evil thoughts of his former
friend; he felt that Selwyn was a selfish,
heartless fellow from skin to skin. Moreover, the look of suspicion, as well as dread,
that his wife had cast upon him, when
Walter had said that he who would keep
back the document would be almost as
guilty as Corralli himself, had not been lost
upon him; it seemed to imply, not indeed
that Sir Reginald had done such a thing,
but that the person who knew him best
conceived it possible that he might be
capable of doing it. These thoughts
crowded upon him as he sat alone in his
little chamber waiting for news from this
man; there was no relief to them, unless
the picture of Lilian wasted to a shadow, as
he had seen her last, but with her beautiful
eyes lacking the light of reason, could be
called a relief. When an hour had thus
passed by, he could bear it no longer;
inaction had become intolerable to him, and
he once more bent his steps towards the hotel.
His importunity seemed to have been anticipated, for no sooner had he again in-

quired for Sir Reginald than he was informed that the baronet had stepped out, but had left a message to the effect that "he had nothing further to communicate to Mr. Litton." As he left the door, the gun at the observatory announced to the townsfolk sunset—to him, that one day of the allotted four he had yet to live had expired.

CHAPTER VII.

A GLEAM OF HOPE.

T was too late that night to call upon the consul or the bankers, on whom indeed his mind misgave him it would be of small use to call in any case; but a sudden impulse caused him to seek the gate of the English burial-ground. Even if Santoro were there, he could obviously afford him no assistance; and it was to the last degree improbable that he should be there, on that first evening of their arrival, and when he might naturally conclude that the young Englishman would have no need to see him. Yet he went on the bare chance of his being there. His heart seemed to yearn for the one companion with whom, if he had no sympathy, he had at least something in

common, who shared with him that knowledge of his own perilous position which it
seemed impossible to induce any one else in
Palermo to share. The broker's man who
sits in possession of the poor man's goods
may not take pity upon him, but he knows
the sad fact of the position, and is so far
preferable to the friend who ignores his
ruin, or disbelieves it, and would fain have
him shout and sing.

Finding Santoro at the spot agreed upon,
"Why, you could hardly have expected to
see me so soon?" said he.

"I did not expect it, signor; but I had
my orders not to lose a chance of communi-
cating with you."

"Indeed! It struck me that the captain
did not trouble himself much about the
matter."

"It was not the captain; it was la
signora," answered the other significantly.

Walter felt the colour come into his
cheeks, as he replied as carelessly as he
could : "But you are not one of la signora's
men; I understood that only those two
who came up from the cavern were under
her directions."

" That is so, signor ; but one that is dear to her is very dear to me."

" Ah ! Lavocca?"

" Yes, signor. I would go through fire and water to serve her," answered he simply. " Have you any news ?"

" Bad news. It is that I wished to see you about. The authorization which Mr. Brown sent for the payment of the ransom is not to be found. Are you sure that no one could have possessed himself of it, while the English lady was being brought back ?"

Santoro shook his head. " That is impossible. In the first place, it would have benefited no one ; and in the second, no one would have dared."

" That is also my opinion. But at all events, it has disappeared, and without it I fear not a ducat can be raised. My idea is, that you should return at once to the camp, and bring back another order from Mr. Brown."

" But that would be very dangerous, signor."

" How so, when the troops have been withdrawn ?"

"Oh, the troops are nothing; it is Corralli himself that I should fear to meet. It is contrary to his wishes that we came down here: his patience is already exhausted, and he would not believe one word of such a tale as this. My return, I feel confident, would be the signal for putting Milord to death at once. You don't know the captain's temper, signor. And then there is Corbara to egg him on. Of course I will go if such is your wish, but that is my conviction."

In vain Walter attempted to move Santoro from this opinion, delivered with all the gravity of a judge *in banco.* It was certain that he was in the best position to speak positively upon such a matter; and he had no motive for misrepresenting it. Walter felt convinced, against his will, that upon himself alone depended the success of his mission. Yet without the authorization, how could he hope to induce the bankers to advance such a sum, or the tenth part of it? To be sure he had Mr. Brown's credentials in the paper he had given him at parting, which begged them to put confidence in the bearer, and to hasten matters as much as possible; but what was the tag of the play without the play itself? If the sum had been a thousand pounds, or even five thousand, it might easily enough have been raised under such an urgent necessity; but fifty thousand pounds! He felt that the task he was about to undertake was almost hopeless, but yet he must needs attempt it by whatever means he found available. He shook hands with Santoro, and returned alone to his own lodgings. Francisco met him at the door with, for him, quite extravagant signs of welcome and satisfaction.

"I never thought to see your face again, signor," exclaimed he. "I was right, you see, about these gentlemen of the mountains. Well, you have seen Corralli face to face, and yet escaped him with a whole skin and a whole purse. That is what no other man in Sicily can say for himself, save you and me."

Walter did not think it worth while to undeceive him; he was resolutely bent upon returning to the brigands, but he did not wish to be made out a martyr, nor even, as Sir Reginald called him, a madman, for so doing: he felt that his own opinion and

that of the world as to what was right to
be done would be at variance, and he did
not wish to discuss the matter.

"Then the young lady too," continued
Francisco with quite unwonted loquacity;
"she has reason to thank her stars, for
it is better to be ill in Palermo than to
enjoy the best of health up yonder," and he
pointed towards Mount Pelegrino, "without
a roof to one's head, and among bad company. They say that Joanna is a she-
devil."

"Then they do her a great injustice,
Francisco," answered Walter gravely. "But
how did you know that the lady had been
with Joanna?"

"Oh, well, there is a friend of mine, a
young woman at the hotel, who has no
secrets from me, and, as it so happens, she
is the signora's nurse for the present."

"But did the signora tell her, then?"

"I suppose so. Who else? Certainly
she told her."

"But Sir Reginald himself informed me
that she was delirious—not capable of
understanding what was said to her."

"I believe that is so. She chatters on,

poor thing—so Julia tells me—by the hour together. Can you guess one particular person whom she talks about, signor?" The boy looked roguishly up in Walter's face. "Ah, I say to Julia, when you go out of your mind you will talk of me, as your mistress talks of Signor Litton."

Under other circumstances this piece of information would have had an interest for Walter absorbing enough—though indeed by that time he possessed the full assurance that Lilian loved him—but there was something else the lad had dropped which riveted his attention even more.

"Then, when the lady first came back to Palermo," returned he anxiously, "she was aware of all that had happened to her? It is only lately that she has lost consciousness. Is that so, Francisco?"

"I believe so. I will ask Julia if you like when I see her next."

"By all means ask her. But when will you see her?"

"Perhaps to-morrow, perhaps not till the day after; it depends upon the signora's state whether she can get away or not. But the next time she shall give me all particulars: you may look upon the matter as settled."

This information moved Walter greatly, as corroborating his worst suspicions, for if it should turn out to be correct, it must needs follow that there was foul-play on the baronet's part with respect to the concealment of the authorization, or at all events of Lilian's mission. She would hardly have spoken of her imprisonment and of Joanna without mentioning the very purpose to effect which she had obtained her freedom.

The next morning, as soon as business hours commenced, Walter presented himself at the British consul's, and told his story, to which that official listened with attentive courtesy. Nothing, however, he said, could be done so far as he was concerned, more than had already been done. The authorities at Palermo had acted promptly, and as duty plainly pointed out to them, in sending forth the troops; and all that he could do, if it was indeed the case that they had been withdrawn, would be to demand that they should make another attempt to compel the brigands to surrender their captive. As to the ransom, it was not to be expected that the Sicilian Government would assist in its collection, or even countenance its payment. That was a matter for the consideration of Mr. Brown's bankers.

All this Walter felt to be perfectly reasonable; but what secretly galled him was, that beneath all this polite logic he could plainly perceive a profound incredulity, not indeed in his story, but in the reality of Corralli's threat. It was evident that the consul had not become acclimatized, but still believed the personal safety of a British merchant to be invincible even from a brigand. That Mr. Brown might be shot in a skirmish he believed to be probable enough; but that he should be put to death in cold blood, was something out of the region of possibility. Walter congratulated himself that he had made no mention of his own peril, since he felt that his anxiety would in that case have been set down to an exaggerated sense of personal danger. At the English banker's, to which the consul was civil enough to accompany him, he was admitted to an interview with one of the members of the firm, and at once presented Mr. Brown's memorandum— "Spare no expense; trust implicitly the bearer."

"Bearer!" repeated the man of money; "why, this is almost as bad as a blank cheque."

Here the consul interposed with a few hurried words in Sicilian, which though he caught their meaning but indistinctly, made Walter flush with indignation. He perceived he was indebted to that gentleman's good offices for convincing Mr. Gordon that he was really the person indicated in the document.

"You see, sir, this is a matter of business," explained the banker; "and when we are asked to put implicit confidence in a man we like to be sure it is the right man. It seems unlike a man of business such as Mr. Brown that he should have written such a memorandum at all."

"If you were half-starved, and surrounded by brigands with cocked pistols, sir, you would not be so scrupulous about technicalities," observed Walter, still a little sore at the nature of his reception.

" We are well aware of Mr. Brown's misfortune, and regret it deeply," answered the banker with stiffness ; " but still the form" —and again he looked at the slip of paper suspiciously—" is unusual."

" It is, however, but the corollary of a document that should have been long ago in your hands, Mr. Gordon—an authorization for the payment of three hundred thousand ducats as ransom."

" Three hundred thousand ducats !" exclaimed the banker. " Why, that is preposterous !"

" No doubt it appears so ; yet, if one possessed the money, one would, I suppose, give it to save one's life." And with that Walter once more told his story.

It was plain the banker was much moved, for he had lived much longer in Sicily than the consul, and therefore knew more of brigands.

" Well, it is a huge sum," he said ; " and to raise it within so short a time we shall require help from the other banks, which, however, will no doubt assist us in such an emergency. Mr. Christopher Brown has no account with us to speak of, but his name is no doubt a good one. It will be a great risk, and yet one which, under the circumstances, it may be our duty to run."

Walter felt as though this man were giving him new life ; he had heard and had believed that money could not save men from death, but here was an instance to the contrary.

" However, no step can of course be taken in the matter without the production of the authorization," continued the banker.

" Alas, sir, I have told you that it cannot be found."

" But if it is not found, Mr. Litton, it must surely be plain to you that you are taking up my time to no purpose. Not that I grudge it to you, under the circumstances; but you cannot be serious in expecting us to raise a fortune upon such a security as *this*"—and he held out the slip of paper between his finger and thumb, in a very hopeless manner—"for an almost total stranger."

" Then God help us !" said Walter.

" In what relation do you stand towards Mr. Brown, young gentleman ?" asked the banker, struck by the earnestness of this reply.

" I am only his friend, sir, and his fellow-sufferer."

" But I understood that he had relatives with him."

" He has two daughters—one of them, as I have told you, seriously, I fear dangerously, ill—and a son-in-law, Sir Reginald Selwyn."

" But surely it was his duty to have accompanied you here to-day;" and once more, as it seemed to Walter, there came into the banker's face that look of distrust with which he had first greeted the presentation of his credentials.

" Sir Reginald is not aware of my visit to you, Mr. Gordon, nor even of my possession of this paper. I came straight from Mr. Brown himself, who had no reason to doubt that the authorization was in your hands."

" Let it be searched for thoroughly, Mr. Litton. If it is not found, you must perceive for yourself how utterly futile is any application to our firm."

" Forgive me, sir, for having taken up so much of your time," said Walter, rising; " that I was pleading the cause of a dying man—one whose life, that is, is as good as lost if this money be not paid— must be my excuse."

He said not a word concerning his own peril, nor indeed at the moment did it occupy his thoughts. The hardness, if not the villany, of Sir Reginald; the misery of Lotty; the pitiable condition of poor Lilian, unable to speak a word upon a subject so vital to her father; the old merchant's impending fate—all these things oppressed Walter's mind, and made the world by no means a place that he felt loth to quit. The despondency and despair in the young man's face touched the banker's heart.

"Search, I repeat, Mr. Litton, for this authorization," said he more kindly, as he held out his hand; "but if it cannot be found, still come to me again, to-morrow at latest. Indeed, we will do for you what we can."

With which poor gleam of hope, Walter took his leave.

CHAPTER VIII.

A LAST APPEAL.

HEN death is drawing nigh us, we do not blink at the truth of matters as when we have time to toy with it; and Walter who, though so young and strong, was yet—if he kept his word—upon life's brink, felt his own mind convinced that even if the authorization still existed, it would not be permitted to leave the hands that held it, since those hands (he felt equally sure) were Reginald Selwyn's. Yet not the less on that account did it behove him to do his best to obtain it. It was a bitter humiliation to have to make application to this man once again, and the more so because to him, and him alone, he had confided that his own life was imperilled as well as that of Mr. Brown;

but for the latter's sake he was resolved to
do so. He accordingly called at the baronet's
hotel to request another interview. The
reply brought to him by the servant was
that Sir Reginald had not yet risen. He
called again an hour afterwards, and found
that he had gone out. As Walter had left
a pressing message on the first occasion, and
since his own lodgings were only a few
paces from the hotel, it was now evident to
him that Sir Reginald intended to avoid
him. He therefore sat down and wrote a
letter, in which he once more urged the
immense importance of the document with
which Lilian had been entrusted; stated his
firm belief that it had not been lost upon
the way into the town; and adjured him, if
he wished to save his father-in-law from a
cruel death, that he should use every effort
to discover it. "If it indeed be lost," wrote
he, "you can certify to that effect, and your
personal presence at the banker's, may, even
as it is, be of some avail." He added this
in case Sir Reginald had destroyed the
paper from unwillingness to let so large a
slice out of the family fortune be sacrificed,
rather than with the actual intention of

benefiting himself by the merchant's death ; or to give him opportunity of repentance and reparation if he had indeed contemplated so great a crime. To this letter, and not until late in the evening, a verbal answer was delivered at Walter's lodgings, to the effect that Sir Reginald had nothing to add to what he had already communicated to Mr. Litton. The method and terms of this reply struck Walter as being equally suspicious ; it seemed to him that the baronet was not only resolved not to commit himself to paper, but that he had purposely avoided any direct reference to the authorization itself. Should Lilian recover, there would therefore be no direct evidence (except from Lotty, which was as good as none) that the document had ever been inquired for at his hands ; while if she died—the merchant and himself having fallen victims to Corralli— Sir Reginald would only have to account to his own conscience for his share in the transaction. At the same time, Walter felt that it would be useless to make public this terrible suspicion that had not indeed sprung up in his own mind in a single night, for it had its roots in long experience, but which must seem to others of monstrous and abnormal growth.

The first thing on the morrow, agreeably to the invitation he had received, Walter once more presented himself at the English bank. Mr. Gordon welcomed him with much kindness, and he fancied that there was a smile of something like assurance on his face, as well as welcome.

"Well, sir, and have you found this authorization?" were his first words.

"No, Mr. Gordon; and I frankly tell you that I think it will not be found."

"But who could have taken it? Of what use would it be to any human being, save to Mr. Brown himself and this rascal Corralli, whose people would be therefore the last to have stolen it?"

"I cannot say, sir," replied Walter gloomily; a reply that expressed the state of the case more literally than his interlocutor imagined. He could indeed make a shrewd guess of what use it might be to a certain person, but he could not say so. "I can only repeat that it is not to be found."

"Well, this is very unfortunate, because

it would have made matters comparatively easy," answered Mr. Gordon. "I have, however, been in communication with my partners on the matter, and they are willing, under the very exceptional circumstances of the case, to make an exceptional effort. We cannot treat, of course, with you as a principal; but if Mr. Brown's son-in-law and daughter will come to us in person, prepared to make an affidavit respecting this document, and to execute a deed guaranteeing us against the loss of the money, it shall be raised by to-morrow morning. It is most unfortunate that Mr. Brown's other daughter should be ill, but we must take her acquiescence for granted."

Mr. Gordon evidently imagined that he was not only making a very generous offer, which in truth he was, but also one which would be greedily accepted by the parties concerned; and the gloom that still overshadowed Walter's face irritated him not a little.

"If such an arrangement does not come up to your ideas of what is liberal, Mr. Litton," said he sharply, "they will differ

very much from those of the commercial
world, I promise you."

"Your offer, Mr. Gordon, is most liberal,
most generous—I acknowledge it with all
my heart; but I am doubtful if it will be
of any service. Sir Reginald Selwyn told
me that even should the authorization be
found, it would be a question with him
whether he should make use of it. As a
matter of principle, he said he objected to
treat with brigands at all, except with the
sword; and as for a guarantee, it is my firm
impression that he will never give it."

"Indeed, indeed," said the banker
thoughtfully. "This is then a very serious
business, for if Sir Reginald positively
refuses to execute the deed I spoke of, we
can do nothing. At the same time, I
cannot think that he will venture to refuse
in the teeth of public opinion. People will
not hesitate to say that he let his father-in-
law be put to death, in order that—his wife
being, as we conclude, co-heiress—he might
inherit his money."

"My belief is, Mr. Gordon," answered
Walter gravely, "that he will let people
say what they please."

There was a short pause, during which the banker regarded him with fixed attention.

"You have had no quarrel with Sir Reginald, I presume, sir?" inquired he presently.

"There has been no absolute quarrel, but we are certainly not on good terms. I must confess I have no good opinion of him."

"Well, I am glad to hear that, because I hope you are judging him harshly. Go to him at once, and state the case exactly as it stands. Here are his father-in-law's bankers prepared to advance this ransom upon the guarantee of himself and Lady Selwyn, and on the understanding that Miss Lilian Brown, on her recovery, and in case of anything going wrong with the money, will join with her sister in seeing us righted."

"Of that I will be answerable with my life—that is, if my life were worth anything," added Walter hastily, his thoughts mechanically recurring to the brigand camp.

"Well, certainly, your life would not be a very convertible commodity, Mr. Litton," answered the banker, smiling, "although I am sure it is a valuable one. I hope to see more of you before you leave Palermo, and under more pleasant circumstances. Above all, I hope to see you again to-day, and accompanied by Sir Reginald and Lady Selwyn."

Directly he understood that the baronet and Walter had quarrelled, it was obvious that Mr. Gordon took a less serious view of the matter, and had little apprehension of any serious obstacle on Sir Reginald's part.

"I will do my very best, sir," answered Walter earnestly; "and whatever happens, I thank you from the bottom of my heart. Good-bye, Mr. Gordon."

"Nay! don't let us say 'good-bye,' but 'good-day,' said the banker, shaking hands with him, and accompanying him to the door. "On Tuesday we have a little dinner-party, and, if you will allow me, I will send you a card of invitation to your lodgings."

A card of invitation for Tuesday! Never, perhaps, did such a simple act of courtesy awaken such bitter thoughts as those which filled Walter's mind as he took his way home through the crowded streets. All about him was full of light and life, but upon his inmost heart the shadow of death had already fallen. His firm conviction was that his fate was sealed, and that no Tuesday would ever dawn upon him in this world. He would do his best with Sir Reginald of course—though his best should include no word of appeal upon his own account; if his own life alone had been in peril, he would not have stooped to ask it of him at all—but he had an overwhelming presentiment that his visit would be fruit-less.

At the hotel door he was met, as usual, by the statement that Sir Reginald was not within.

"It is no matter ; I will go in and wait for him," was Walter's quiet rejoinder ; and there was a determination in his tone which it was not in Sicilian nature—or, at all events, in the nature of a Sicilian hotel porter—to resist. He walked upstairs, and entered the sitting-room of the baronet without announcement.

Lotty was seated there alone, and thinking no doubt that it was her husband, she did not even look up from her employment. Her back was turned towards him, and she was engaged, or appeared to be so, upon some sort of needle-work, but he noticed that she passed her handkerchief rapidly across her eyes as he entered the room.

"Lady Selwyn," said he, "forgive this intrusion, but my business admits of no delay."

She sprang to her feet, and faced him with a frightened look.

"Oh, Mr. Litton, does Reginald know——" She hesitated, and he could see she trembled in every limb.

"That I am here?" answered Walter quietly. "No; he does not know it, but it is necessary he should do so. I am come on an errand of the greatest moment, and one on which hangs your father's life."

"O, sir, you must be mistaken," replied she, her eyes filling with tears: "it cannot be so bad as that. Reginald assures me that it cannot."

"Your husband cannot know the facts, Lady Selwyn, as I know them. To-morow will be your father's last day on earth, unless one of two things happens. One is, that the authorization which your sister brought with her from the brigands' camp into this house shall be forthcoming."

" I cannot find it; I have searched everywhere ; indeed, indeed I have," returned she earnestly.

" Perhaps Sir Reginald could find it, if he tried."

Lotty's pale face assumed an awful whiteness, and her teeth began to chatter as though with cold.

" No, Mr. Litton, he cannot," she gasped. " It is lost, lost, lost !"

" You mean, that I am too late," said Walter sternly—" that it has been destroyed."

" I don't say that, I don't say that !" cried Lady Selwyn passionately. " I did not see him do it; but yet, in ignorance of its importance, he may have done it. What was the other hope—the other chance? O help me, help me, Mr. Litton, to save my father !"

" The other hope—and the only other hope—lies in yourself."

" In *me !*" exclaimed she joyfully ; " then he is saved."

"In you, and in your husband." The light faded from her eyes in a moment, and she uttered a deep sigh. "Yes; you and he have only to present yourselves at the English bank this day, and execute a certain deed, and the ransom will be paid."

"I will ask him, Mr. Litton; I will beseech him; but you know" (here she smiled a wretched smile) "that I have not much power; and he is so convinced—being a soldier, you see, himself—that the better way is to send the troops. Perhaps—he will be very angry, I am afraid, to find you here—but still, perhaps you will not mind seeing him yourself."

"I shall most certainly see him myself, Lady Selwyn."

"And do not give him an opportunity for quarrel," continued Lotty earnestly; "for my father's sake, and for Lilian's, be careful of that. Bear with him, Mr. Litton."

"I will endeavour to do so," answered Walter gravely. Her advice was good so far as it went; for it was likely enough that Sir Reginald would endeavour to escape what was required of him by means of a quarrel ; but, then, was it not still more probable that he would contrive to quarrel in any case?

"How is Lilian?" inquired Walter. "You may imagine the pressing importance of my visit here, since I have not put that question before. The porter in the hall, however, informed me that she is much the same."

"No ; she is better," said Lotty, dropping her voice, and looking cautiously round; "I can give you that much comfort. She is herself again—quite herself—though of course as weak as a child."

"Ah! if it were ten days hence, instead of to-morrow—to-morrow!" murmured Walter involuntarily.

"Why so, Mr. Litton?"

"Because Lilian herself could have then gone to the bankers'; but at present that would of course be out of the question."

"O yes, quite. In three days' time, however, I think she would be strong enough to see you—and I am sure it would please her."

"In three days' time! This woman had already then forgotten," thought he, "the

11—2

fate that awaited her father within less than
forty-eight hours. What a weak and wavering nature was hers, how impressionable, and
yet how easily every impression was effaced!
How could it have been possible that there
had been a time—and not so long ago—
when he had thought of her as one of the
noblest of womankind! How different and
how inferior was she to his Lilian!"

This was somewhat hard on Lotty, for
she had not forgotten what Walter had
told her respecting her father, only she did
not think matters were quite so bad as he
described. She believed him more than she
believed her husband, but it was natural
that she should believe the latter a little—not
that she did not know him to be untruthful,
but because she was loth to think of him
so ill, as it would be necessary to do if
Walter were right in his forebodings. She
had also the tendency of her sex, to think
all risks much less than they were
represented to be.

" I suppose," said Walter, not without a
tremulousness in his tone, " that it would
not be possible for me to see Lilian either
to-day or to-morrow morning, even for a

few minutes ?" It seemed so hard to go to
the grave without bidding her good-bye,
though he knew it would cost him so
much; as for her, it would cost her nothing
in that respect, since it would be dangerous
as well as useless to tell her how matters
really stood.

" Well, you might see *her*," said Lotty
hesitating; "but I could hardly promise
that she could see *you*. Perhaps the day
after to-morrow, when she has had her
afternoon sleep and is at her best, she
might bear the interview. She has often
spoken of you, and even asked for you,
though sometimes I doubted whether she
knew what she was saying; and considering
what you have undergone together, I cannot
think there can be any harm—and Reginald
has said nothing against it—yes, I really
do think we might say the day after
to-morrow."

It was almost a relief to Walter, finding
poor Lotty what she was, to hear Sir
Reginald's stern voice in the hall (doubtless
rebuking the porter for having given his
visitor admittance), and to feel that from
him he would at least definitely know his

fate. It was easy to see by Lady Selwyn's face that she heard it also.

"Shall I go, Mr. Litton," murmured she hurriedly, "or shall I stay? If you think I can be of any use——" It was evident enough which alternative the poor lady preferred, and Walter was disinclined to put her to pain; moreover, it was as likely that the presence of a witness would harden Sir Reginald in his villany—if villany he intended to commit—as that it would shame him into propriety; and again, if the baronet proved obstinate, Walter would be compelled, for her sake, to mitigate the indignation and contempt which in that case he was fully resolved to express towards him.

"It is just as well I should see your husband alone, Lady Selwyn," said he gently; and Lotty disappeared through one door as Sir Reginald presented himself at the other. "It seems to me, Mr. Litton, that you are very importunate," were his first words, as he closed the door carefully behind him. Neither the action nor the unaccustomed pallor of the baronet's face escaped his visitor. They were evidences to him that this man had made up his mind upon the matter in hand, but at the same time was ashamed of his resolution, or at all events was well aware that disgrace would be imputed to him.

"Where two men's lives are in such imminent peril, Sir Reginald, I do not think that any endeavour to save them should be termed importunity. The authorization entrusted to your sister-in-law's hands has, it seems, been lost."

"You have already had your answer upon that point," replied the other coldly. "As to its being 'lost,' indeed, I cannot say, because that supposes such a document to have been in existence; but, at all events, it has not been found."

"And I conclude, Sir Reginald, I may take it for granted that it will not be found?"

"I do not understand you, Mr. Litton."

But it was plain by the red spot on his cheekbones, and the hard glitter of his eyes, that he was well aware of what was meant.

"We are quite alone, Sir Reginald," said Walter in firm significant tones, "and there is no reason why I should not speak plainly. The loss of this document, I must needs remind you, which includes also the sacrifice of your father-in-law's life, would be to you a great gain. It behoves you therefore, for your reputation's sake, if for no better reason, to——"

"My reputation, sir," interrupted Sir Reginald contemptuously, "can stand any slur which Mr. Walter Litton may choose to cast upon it."

"I do not speak of myself, I am merely quoting the opinion of Mr. Gordon, the banker here, which will, I am sure, be shared by every one of our countrymen in this place, that if you refuse to assist in rescuing Mr. Brown from the cruel hands which threaten him, your conduct will be open to the gravest suspicions. The money which it is well known you would inherit by such a course of proceeding, would doubtless be a consideration—but it would be blood money."

Sir Reginald was trembling with rage in every limb, but yet he restrained himself, as Walter knew he could never have done had he been imputing to him less than the truth. "It is certainly very agreeable, Mr.

Litton," said he, in a hoarse voice, "to find that others beside yourself are interesting themselves so much in my private affairs; but it is just as well—if they are to be made public—that the facts should be thoroughly understood. You accuse me of concealing or destroying—for it comes to that—a certain document, the very existence of which I do not hesitate to deny. It is true my sister-in-law has mentioned the very sum you speak of—the monstrous amount of which, by-the-bye, seemed well to consort with her unhappy condition—but as to seeing it stated in black and white, that nobody has done. Yet because I don't produce it, you go about the town, it seems, accusing me of refusing to assist my father-in-law in obtaining his freedom. I have done my best—and in accordance with the judgment of those best fitted to advise in such matters—by getting the troops sent out, and I am prepared to do aught else— short of what is utterly unreasonable—to further the same end."

"In that case, then, Sir Reginald," said Walter gravely, "my object in coming here to-day is accomplished. I am commissioned by Mr. Gordon to inform you, that if you and Lady Selwyn will present yourselves in person at the bank to-day, that your guarantees for the money will be accepted in place of the authorization, and that in that case Mr. Brown's ransom will be forthcoming at once."

" What! the three hundred thousand ducats ?"

For the moment astonishment had dulled Sir Reginald's wits; instead of being ready with an excuse for not conforming to this unexpected offer, he could only oppose an incredulity which the facts must needs overcome. The idea of his personal guarantee being accepted for such a sum as fifty thousand pounds—one hundredth part of which in ready money he had rarely possessed in his life—had utterly overwhelmed him.

Walter began to think that his own difficulties were over, and ventured to smooth away those which seemed to present themselves to Sir Reginald.

" Your guarantee," said he, " it is true will be but a matter of form. When Mr. Brown regains his liberty, he will of course

be glad enough to pay the money; only, in
the absence of the authorization, the bank
needs to be assured of this, by his daughter
and yourself."

" But if he does not regain his liberty,
and the money is taken by the brigands all
the same?" observed the baronet. "Supposing even they were to kill him—as you
have told me is possible—and these three
hundred thousand ducats go into Corralli's
pockets all the same?"

" That is to the last degree improbable;
such a breach of faith has never been known
among these people."

" Improbable! But is it impossible?
that is the question. As to honour among
thieves, to be sure there is a proverb to that
effect, but it would scarcely justify me, I
should imagine, in putting such a temptation as fifty thousand pounds in the way of
a Sicilian brigand. No, Mr. Litton; I am
sensible—you may tell Mr. Gordon—of the
compliment he pays me; but I must decline
to accept such a responsibility—to undertake
an obligation which I have no means of discharging—should things turn out amiss—as
a man of honour."

"I must again remind you that we are quite alone, Sir Reginald," said Walter bitterly, "and that I know you perfectly well. You have undertaken obligations before now which you had much less chance of discharging than this one, and with much less important objects. Your scruples upon this matter, when I saw you last, and when no such opportunity as the present offered itself, were confined to making overtures to the brigands at all, who you said must be treated with, on principle, by the sword alone. Those scruples, it seems, you have forgotten; but you have found others more adapted for the new conditions. I do not doubt that in any case you would find reasons enough to excuse you from following the course which duty and humanity alike point out to you. As for me—if you persist in this wickedness—I shall be a dead man to-morrow night; but do not imagine that I shall die unavenged. I will leave behind me a statement of your conduct in this matter towards your relative, which, so soon as the news comes of our double murder, shall be published far and wide. You will be rich perhaps, for it is possible—

I have no doubt you are speculating upon
her illness turning out fatally even now—
that you may obtain poor Lilian's inheri-
tance as well as that of your wife; but you
will never purchase, I do not say the respect,
but the recognition of your fellow-creatures.
You will be held as a man accursed. That
you are brave—in one sense, at all events—
I am well aware; but you will not be brave
enough to hold up your head when the
finger of public scorn is pointed at it!"

" Have you done—have you quite done?"
inquired Sir Reginald coldly. " Have you
any more theatrical effects with which to
favour me?"

" 1 have nothing more to say, Reginald
Selwyn, except to put the question for the
last time: Will you stir a finger to save
your father-in-law's life, or will you
not?"

"If you mean by stirring a finger, will
I become a party to a negotiation with
brigands?—no; I will not!"

" Mr. Gordon was right," said Walter
bitterly, as he rose from his chair. " There
was a time when Reginald Selwyn was a
gentleman and a soldier; but I know him

now for what, in his cruel heart, he knows himself to be, a scoundrel and an assassin!"

Sir Reginald leaped to his feet, but the passion which, in the days that Walter had referred to, would have prompted him to strike his adversary to the earth, gave way immediately to calculations of prudence. He reflected that a conflict with his quondam friend at such a time would be most damaging to his interests and reputation. Walter waited quietly for the expected assault—in truth, he desired nothing better than to grapple with his enemy, with little solicitude for what might be the result of such an encounter ; but perceiving that it was not to happen, uttered but one word, "Coward!" and looking steadily in the other's face, turned on his heel and left the room.

CHAPTER IX.

 GREAT poetess has described for us the aspects under which death appears to man in his various ages; but the welcome which but too many of us are ready to give it, she has forborne to sing. There are many thousands in this little land of ours, I do not doubt, who would receive with joy a summons to eternal peace, if it were only to be cessation from trouble, and nothing more. For such indeed the idea of heaven is far too high, as that of hell is far too monstrous. Only to rest and to be out of the world is their piteous desire. It is probable that the establishment of life-assurance societies has prolonged human existence more than all the appliances of science before and since

their era. There is many a man for whom
not only Prosperity and Pleasure are over,
but even Hope itself, who feels not only old
age and poverty and care growing over him
like mosses upon a wall—though, alas, not
so painlessly—but comfortless despair; there
is many a man, I say, who if himself were
alone concerned in the matter, would certainly end all with a bare bodkin, without
much fear of the after-dream. It is true,
indeed, that what we fear is worse than
what we feel; but the feeling is in this case
sharp and sensible, while the fear is vague
and shadowy. With what bitter but secret
smiles do church-going men often listen to
homilies about the joys of life, and the
eager clutch with which humanity clings to
it! Still doubtless, on the whole, the poet
is right; to most men—let us thank God for
it—life is dear. To the young it is especially
so, for to them, even if it may sometimes
seem that it would be well to die, the
Preacher's words are true, that heaviness
may endure for a night, but joy cometh in
the morning. Thus, as we have seen, it
had lately appeared to Walter Litton that
existence had no great boon to offer him,

and that he might let go his hold upon it
without much regret ; but now that he was
standing in the shining street, with the sea
one smile before him, and the voices and
laughter of his fellow-men breaking in upon
his ear, it again seemed hard to die. He
was not yet three-and-twenty, and in perfect
health and vigour ; the slight hurt that his
few days of scarcity and exposure upon the
mountains had done him, or perhaps had
only seemed to do him, was quite passed
away. There was no reason—save that
terrible bail-bond of his word he had given
to the brigand chief, and which was to be
exacted on the morrow—why he should not
live for the next fifty years ; breathe the
soft air, feel the warm sun, gaze into the
pure depths of yonder sky, and eat and
drink and be merry with his fellows. If
only that little promise of his could be
blotted from his mind—and only from his
own mind, for no one else would reproach
him for breaking it—he felt that his life
might be a happy one. Should Lilian recover, of which there now seemed to be
good hope, she would undoubtedly accept
him for her husband, in spite of any repre-

sentations of Sir Reginald. To have love, riches, health, and youth within his power, and yet to exchange all to-morrow—to-morrow—for a cruel and lingering death, was a terrible thought indeed.

The contrast did not, however, present itself in the form of a temptation. He did not need to picture to himself the disappointment of the unhappy old merchant at his non-appearance in the brigand camp, nor the mortification of Joanna at that evidence of his want of faith; indeed, they would both, he knew, be glad that he had thus escaped his doom, since it was to be escaped no other way; nor did the thought of the bitter triumph of Corralli over his broken word affect him in the least, for it never entered into his mind to break his word. He was going back on the morrow to his death, as he had always intended to do, should things turn out as they had done; but he had not expected them so to turn out; and his disappointment was very bitter, and his regrets very keen. He had no sense of any heroism in his own conduct, but only of the hardness of the fate that necessitated it; and he was furious against

the selfish and murderous greed of Sir
Reginald. If religion required of him in
that hour of wretchedness to forgive the
man who, if not the actual cause of it, had
by his criminal inaction conduced to it,
Walter was not religious ; he hated and
despised him infinitely more than Corralli
himself, and in all the dark turmoil of his
thoughts kept this one clear and distinct
before him—that so far as in him lay,
Reginald Selwyn should not escape un-
punished. There are many good and wise
axioms that require to be acted upon with
a difference, according to the character of
those with whom we have to deal. A soft
answer we are told, for example, turneth
away wrath ; and it doubtless does so in
many cases ; but there are others in which
conciliation is not only thrown away, but
increases the fury of the wicked man, since
he conceives from it that he may be furious
with impunity. Another excellent precept
is to leave evil-doers to the punishment of
their own conscience ; but here also it is
necessary to be convinced that in the particular case such an instrument of chastisement exists. To have left Reginald Selwyn

to the stings of remorse, would have been
much the same as to have inflicted a fine of
five shillings upon a millionaire for murder.
Walter was firmly resolved to inflict no fine
upon him, but such a penalty as he must
needs feel. He therefore made use of one
of the few hours of life remaining to him to
draw up a detailed statement of the facts of
Mr. Christopher Brown's capture and imprisonment, with especial reference to the
ransom which would have procured his release; the mysterious disappearance of the
authorization, and Sir Reginald's lukewarm-
ness concerning it; the negotiations with
the banker, and the baronet's refusal to sign
the guarantee : nor did he hesitate to point
out how by such a course of conduct the
latter's material interests had been advan-
taged at the expense of his unhappy relative.
This paper he sealed up and addressed to
the British consul, with a request that it
might be made public so soon as the fatal
news from Corralli's camp should reach
the city. Of himself he said little, beyond
describing the circumstances of his compelled return to the brigands, which would
naturally afford to his statement the weight

which attaches to the evidence of a dying man.

A much more painful, if less important, task then claimed his attention, in bidding farewell to Lilian. It was necessary to do this in writing, since, even if he should have the chance of seeing her (which now seemed improbable), it would have been impossible, in her fragile condition, to communicate to her the true state of the case. He did not waste many words upon Sir Reginald, with whose character he knew Lilian was well acquainted, and of whose conduct in the present matter she would hear the particulars from other sources; but he solemnly laid the fate of her father and himself at the baronet's door, and adjured her to rescue Lotty from his hands, which, as he pointed out, it would be easy to do by making some pecuniary sacrifice. "He has no wish, you will find," he bitterly added, "to keep his captive for her own sake; but in his willingness to accept ransom you will find him the counterpart of Corralli himself." Finally, he asked Lilian's pardon for the involuntary share he had himself taken in the marriage of her

sister with the man who had thus brought
ruin on them all. The rest of his letter
described the steady growth of his affection
for herself, which, although all hope of its
fruition seemed denied to him, had induced
him to come abroad, in the hope of being of
use to her, under circumstances which had
given her just cause for apprehension.
Unhappily his efforts to assist her had
been unavailing, but he besought her to
believe that he in no way regretted
them ; he had done his best and failed ; but
to have done less than his best would have
been a greater pain to him than was his
failure. Then he spoke of their common
youth, and entreated her not tő grieve
unreasonably, or for long, over his decease.
Fate had only permitted them within the
last few days to express to one another their
mutual love ; if he had lived, it was true, it
would have lasted as long as life itself ; but
since he was doomed to die, it was contrary
to nature and reason that her young love
should be wasted on a dead man. He
gave her his full leave—" Such a permission," wrote he, " will seem preposterous
to any other than yourself, but you will feel

that I have the right to give it ; and I fore-
see that it will one day be a relief to you"—
to marry whom she would.   And he wished
her happiness in her wedded life.   Walter
felt that his letter was egotistic ; but also
that she would make allowance—then and
always—for the circumstances under which
it was composed.   The *Ego* was strong
within him.   As he looked out from his
window, earth, sea, and sky seemed to have
the same personal reference to himself that
they have to dying men.   He saw them
now, but after one day more he would never
see them.   The sun was setting, so far as
he was concerned, for the last time save one.
The mighty world, so full of light and life,
would go on as usual, but not for him ; he
was about to drop out of it, and the darkness of the grave to close around him.
After that he knew not what would happen
to him, nor did any man know.   He could
only bow his head in reverent faith.   He
was not afraid of falling into the hands of
God, nor did he repine in an unmanly
manner.   But as he thought of Lilian and
of all that might have been, but which was
not to be, the tears gathered in his eyes.

His mind too wandered back to Beech Street and faithful Jack Pelter. He did not feel equal to writing to him, but he would learn all that had taken place, and he could trust him to construe all aright, so far as he was himself concerned. By his will, made when he came of age by his lawyer's advice, he had left him—the only friend who had at that time "shown himself friendly"—what property he was possessed of; and it was a comfort to him now to think that, notwithstanding his feckless habits, poor Jack would never want. He had put aside some portion of his ready money to pay for his own interment in the English cemetery (a favourite spot with him), should his body be recovered from the brigands; and the rest he had allotted to Francisco, as the marriage portion of his bride. These, with the letters, he intended to leave out upon the morrow, in order that they might be found after he had left the city. And now all matters having been thus provided for in this world, he was sitting at his open window thinking unutterable things.

"Signor!"—he started, so deep he was

in meditation that he had not heard any one enter his apartment—" signor, I have news for you."

It was Francisco's voice, the tones of which were always musical, but which had acquired of late—born of his new-found love—the tenderness of a brook in June, " which to the leafy woods all night singeth a quiet tune ;" his passion had rendered him sympathetic as well as eloquent. " You have scarcely touched your dinner, my father says ; but you will eat supper when you have heard my tidings. The English young lady is better, still weak and worn, poor soul, and a mere shadow to look at : you must not be frightened at that."

" What ! can she see me, then ?"

" Yes ; she will see you : not to-night, because it is too late, but to-morrow."

" To-morrow !" The very word seemed to sound forlorn and sad as he uttered it. " It will be early, then, I hope, Francisco."

" Yes ; it will be very early. After her night's rest, says Julia, her mistress is at her best and strongest, and she wishes to see you, signor, ah, so eagerly !"

" A thousand thanks, Francisco. You

will find that I have not forgotten this good service."

"Oh, do not speak of that. But you must really eat something; none would think that it was but two days ago that you came back half-starved from the mountains."

A sharp pang ran through Walter's frame; he had been reminded of a thing forgotten—namely, his appointment with Santoro for that evening.

"Come, signor, let me bring you supper."

"Presently, Francisco—in half an hour or so; I have something to do first in the town." He turned back to the window, unwilling to prolong this talk; and Francisco, with an anxious glance at his English friend, and a dubious shake of his fine head, withdrew from the apartment. Immediately afterwards Walter took up his hat, and repaired to the usual rendezvous, where he found Santoro awaiting him. He at once informed the brigand that all hope of obtaining the ransom was at an end, and inquired at what hour it would be necessary to start upon the morrow.

"We should be off before noon," was his

quiet reply, "since it takes much longer to climb a mountain than to descend from it."

"Then I will be here before that hour."

"Hush! Not here, signor, but at the end of the Marina," answered the brigand in low tones. "This place is growing too hot for me; certain inquiries have been made, I find, and it is necessary that I should leave the town to-night."

"You do not suppose, I hope, that it is through anything I have said——"

"No, no; the signor is a man of honour; but he has been watched and followed. A brigand's eyes never deceive him."

Walter could not but think that his companion was mistaken, for not only had he been unconscious of any such espionage, but he knew of none who could have any interest in his coming and going. Still it was obvious that Santoro was uneasy, and since it was unnecessary to prolong the interview, they parted at once. As Walter went back to his lodgings, he cast a glance up to the rooms which the Selwyns occupied at the hotel, and saw Sir Reginald smoking and sipping coffee on the balcony; and as

he was the only man who was likely to take
any note of his proceedings, the brigand's sus·
picion seemed to him more baseless even than
before.　Walter's supper was brought up to
him by Baccari himself, and not, as he had
expected, by Francisco, and the good
lodging-house keeper was unusually silent.
His guest was content, however, to observe
the change without making allusion to it,
since, to be left alone with his own thoughts
was, on that night which was to be his last
on earth, what he most desired.

CHAPTER X.

THE TEMPTER.

SLEEP, Walter had feared, would have been impossible for him, under the circumstances in which Fate had placed him; but Nature, while we are young, is kindly to us, and gave him several hours of refreshing slumber. He welcomed them not only for the forgetfulness they afforded, but because they would give him strength to bear, whatever brigand cruelty might have in store, with such manliness as belonged to him, and above all to support the old merchant as much as possible by the exhibition of a bold front. When Francisco came therefore, as had been agreed upon, at an early hour, to conduct him to the hotel, he found the young Englishman calm and collected, and with even less disquietude in his manner than such an interview as lay before him would have seemed to warrant. Had his own position indeed been less momentous, the circumstances under which he was about to visit Lilian would have been painful and embarrassing enough, nor, perhaps, in that case would he have sought to see her at all. Not only was it in some degree a risk to her as respected her health, but the proceeding itself was clandestine—that is, unknown to Sir Reginald, who after all was, in the absence of her father, her natural guardian and protector. However, it was no time now for the entertainment of any delicate scruples. At the door of the hotel he was left by Francisco in the hands of Julia, a soft-eyed Sicilian, who, since Lilian had not her English maid—for whom there had been no room on board the *Sylphide*—had been appointed to the post of sick-nurse. As she led the way upstairs, and passed the floor occupied by the Selwyns, she answered an inquiring look that rose to Walter's face.

"Sir Reginald is asleep, signor, nor will he rise for the next two hours; but you will see Milady Selwyn."

This was a great relief to Walter, upon
Lilian's account, even more than upon his
own, since Lotty's presence would afford full
authority for his visit; and when, at the
next landing, he found her at the door
waiting to receive him, he felt more kindly
towards her than her weakness had permitted him of late to do. He knew that
she was daring much, in thus admitting
him to her sister's presence, without the
knowledge of her husband, and that to
dare was with her to act against her
nature.

"You will not talk with her long," pleaded
she, "Mr. Litton, will you? Lilian is very
weak and feeble; and, above all things,
refrain from speaking about—about that
matter we were talking of yesterday."

"About your father's peril?"

"Well, about your apprehensions upon
his account; Reginald assures me that
there is no real danger. There is nothing
to be gained by dwelling on it; and if my
sister should share your fears, it would have
a very bad effect upon her."

"You may rely on my prudence, Lady
Selwyn," answered Walter quietly; and

thereupon she led the way into the sick-room. The first appearance of Lilian gave Walter an uncomfortable notion that he had been deceived as to her true condition; she was not "up and dressed," as the phrase goes, it is true, but she was lying on a couch by the open window, attired in a dressing-gown, and looking more like a convalescent than one who had so recently been reported as dangerously ill. The hand which she stretched out to him, indeed, was so thin as to be almost transparent; and the voice with which she welcomed him was well nigh as weak as that which had murmured his name when they parted in Joanna's cavern; but instead of the spot of scarlet that had been burnt upon her pallid cheeks, there was now a rose-pink blush, which was certainly not the flush of fever, though it might have been summoned there by his coming.

"This is better than when we met each other last, Walter," said she, with a sweet smile.

"It is indeed, darling." He could say no more, since the truth was not to be said.

"I long to hear how you got away from

that dreadful place, but they say you must not tell me now." The tears, from the mere consciousness of her weakness, stood in her soft eyes, which also brimmed with love and tenderness. " But one thing you must tell me—about dear papa. When shall I see him, when will he be here?"

Walter hesitated. Should he tell her a lie with his dying lips? or the truth, that must needs kill her?

" You have forgotten, my dear Lily, that the ransom has not been paid," interposed Lotty gently.

" But why is this long delay? How cruel it is to keep poor papa in captivity! He must have been days and days, though I know not how long. Do, dear Walter, hasten it."

" I have done what I can, dearest."

" And you are still doing your best, I am sure. But what is the obstacle?"

" The sum is so very large," said Walter, scarce knowing what words he spoke; it was so pitiful to hear her, so pained with even what she knew, so ignorant of what must needs give her so much greater pain.

"Nay, but surely the bank can raise it. What papa wrote was surely sufficient. I kept it next my heart, as though it had been a letter of your own, Walter."

Walter turned his eyes involuntarily towards Lotty with a mute: "You hear *that?*" but her gaze was fixed upon the floor. If she did not know that her husband had possessed himself of the authorization, he felt sure that she suspected it.

"Is it possible that they refuse to pay it?" inquired Lilian, raising herself in her agitation upon her elbow, then instantly sinking back again through sheer exhaustion. If, when Walter had first entered the room, a hope had risen in his breast that Lilian herself might be made the means of saving two doomed lives, it here fell to rise no more. If he could have seen her earlier, and brought the banker to her bedside, something might perhaps have been accomplished; but as it was he felt all was over. It was manifest that the little strength she had had been already expended in saying those few words. There was nothing for it but to leave her to the short-lived bliss of ignorance.

"The bankers do not refuse to pay it, Lilian, but—but we must have patience."

"Poor dear papa!" sighed Lilian, so softly that none but a lover's ear could have caught the sound. "How wretched he must be among these terrible men! O, Walter, when shall we see him?"

"I shall see him to-day, Lilian," answered Walter solemnly.

"To-day!"—with a slight flush of joy—"that is well indeed. You need not have been afraid to tell me such good tidings. It is bad news, not good, that kills one."

Walter's heart sank low within him at these terrible words; still he made shift to smile upon her.

"Tell him, with my dearest love," she went on, "how I long to see him, and to clasp him in my arms! And tell him that if anything could add to the happiness of such a moment, it will be the thought that you have brought him to me. He will not —he will not wish to keep us asunder now, Walter!"

Then she closed her eyes, and Lotty made a sign to him that he should withdraw.

Walter bent down, and took his last kiss

of Lilian; a faint smile played upon her pale lips as he did so, but they did not part even for a word of farewell; and his bursting heart felt grateful that they did not. He could not have answered her "good-bye" with firmness.

Lotty left the room with him, and as those who watch the sick are wont to do when their invalid has a visitor, inquired of him what he thought of Lilian. "Is she better than you expected, Mr. Litton?"

"She is better than I was led to expect," answered Walter coldly.

Lotty's cheek turned a shade whiter, as she observed, without reference to this reply: "Yet she is still so weak that a breath would blow her away."

"Yes; a breath of ill news. You heard what she said just now. That news will come to-morrow, and then Sir Reginald will have the blood of three innocent persons, instead of two, to answer for."

"O, sir, be pitiful!" cried Lotty, trembling.

"What! pitiful to the man who stole that authorization from yonder sick girl— plucked the father's life from the daughter's bosom! Pitiful to the man who has lied to me about Lilian's health—painting her as out of her mind, lest I should question her, and prove him thief, or use her services to save the doomed! Pitiful to the man——"

"No, Mr. Litton—not to the man; I cannot ask it; but to the woman! Pity *me*, who am his wife."

"I do, I do." The pleading misery of her tearful eyes had quenched his rage. If she had had any hand in deceiving him, it was an unwilling hand, nor had she been thoroughly persuaded of the peril in which her father stood.

"I pity you, Lady Selwyn, from my heart; and if—if I should never see your face again——"

"Oh, Mr. Litton!" she interrupted, "then you cannot forgive me?"

"Yes; I forgive you. A time will come, and soon, when it will be a comfort to you to know as much. Keep all news that comes to-morrow from Lilian's ears, from Lilian's eyes, I charge you. Play the hypocrite with her, for my sake, and for your father's sake."

"I can do that," said Lotty bitterly: "Heaven knows, I am used to that."

Perhaps Walter was wrong to think that
at that moment he of all human creatures
was the most wretched; yet, with Lotty,
wretchedness was but as a cloud which
passes.

"And shall you really see dear papa to-
day?" she went on eagerly.

"Yes; to-day."

"Then you will give him my love too,
with Lilian's, and tell him nothing—
nothing—that——"

"Nothing that will make one daughter
less dear to him than the other, Lady
Selwyn, you may be sure."

"God bless you for that, Walter."

"And God bless *you*, Lotty, that should
have been my sister. Farewell—farewell!"

The hand she held out to him was carried
to his lips, then he turned and went down-
stairs with the slow step that bears a heavy
heart. He had seen the last English face,
save one, that he should ever see—that one
which would meet his own with hopeless
agony depicted on it. He saw it even then,
even while the morning-tide of men was
setting in around him, with looks of pleasure
or of business, and with thoughts for the

morrow, and the next day, and for a year to
come; he saw it, in its woe and disappointment, reflected in the clear wave and the
clear sky; he was with it in that camp
among the mountains before he had left the
city walls behind him, and was a captive
once again before his time.

Francisco brought him his breakfast, but
asked no question concerning his recent
visit to the hotel, an omission which, to
judge by the earnest look with which he
regarded his father's lodger, whenever
Walter's eye was not upon him, was
certainly not owing to any want of personal
interest.

"Has Signor Litton any plans for the
day?" he inquired presently.

"Plans for the day?" repeated Walter,
whose mind was so occupied with the thought
of what the day had in store for him, that
he did not readily understand the question.

"I mean," explained Francisco, "will
you not have a sail in the bay, signor, such
as used to please you? There is a pleasant
breeze afloat, though none on shore; and
we can have the old boat, or for that matter,
the signora would doubtless let you have

the yacht itself: it has lain idle these many days, and will do so, I suppose, till Milord Brown's ransom is paid."

"I suppose so," answered Walter mechanically. There was something in his face which seemed to convince Francisco that questioning would be of no avail, for immediately afterwards he withdrew.

Walter lit his pipe, as he was always wont to do after the morning meal, and sat at his window until the hour of noon; then he took a last look around the room, saw that the letters and the two little packets of money were in a place where they could easily be found, and left the house, walking slowly along the Marina, eastward. Every step he took was away from the habitations of his fellow-men, and was as it were an act of farewell to them. We are wont, and justly, to give honour to those who volunteer to lead "forlorn hopes," and put their lives in extreme peril from shot and steel; but such heroes have at least companions in their noble act, and the excitement of battle, fought under the eyes of their comrades; moreover, though the risk to life is great, there is a secret hope in each man's heart

that he may return alive. Now, Walter
Litton was alone; only one man in all
Palermo—and he an enemy—was cognizant
of the sacrifice he was about to make; and
death was certain. He had already got
within a hundred yards of the end of the
Marina, when he heard footsteps, quick and
heavy, coming behind him, and then his
own name called out in English: " Litton—
Walter Litton." He turned round with
cold surprise (for he knew the voice), and
beheld Reginald Selwyn. He thought that
this man had discovered his interview with
Lilian, and was about to seek a quarrel
with him, though Sir Reginald's face,
albeit it was very grave and unwontedly
pale, showed, in truth, no signs of
anger. •

" What is it that you want with me,
sir?" said Walter slowly.

" I want you not to be a fool, Litton,"
answered the other frankly. " I have been
thinking over what you told me you had
made up your mind to do, in case the
extravagant demands of these villains were
not complied with, and though I did not
believe you then, I believe you now. It

seems to me that you are mad enough for anything."

"I am not mad, sir; though, thanks to you, my lot is a very unhappy one."

"But it need not be so if you will only listen to reason. It cannot surely be your purpose, out of a quixotic sense of honour, to give yourself up to these rascals that they may take your life?"

"I intend to keep my word, Sir Reginald Selwyn."

"In other words, you intend to commit suicide."

"No, sir; it is you and Corralli who will, between you, have murdered me. Some touch of tenderness, born of an ancient friendship, may have moved you to urge me thus; if so, let it move you further. There is time—though there is hardly time—even yet to repent of your baseness, and to procure your father-in-law's ransom. By that means you will save both our lives; but otherwise, the blood of both will be on your head: I call Heaven to witness it."

"That is all rubbish, Litton. I cannot consent to be a party to any arrangement with thieves and robbers such as you propose."

" You mean you will not."

" Well, if you choose to take it that way, I will not."

" Then your refusal is our death-doom, and you know it."

" And your departing thus will be Lilian's death-doom," returned Sir Reginald, " when she comes to know what has happened. If I was the scoundrel that you pretend to believe me, I would say ' Go ;' for Lilian will die if you do so, and my wife will of course inherit her money. But, on the contrary, I entreat you not to go. Only think of the chances you are throwing away. It is true that hitherto I have done my best to oppose your marriage with my sister-in-law ; but I will oppose it no longer."

" And your father-in-law having been put to death—you would add—there will be no other obstacle to it."

" Well, of course, if anything happens to Mr. Brown—mind, I don't say it will—I don't believe it will——"

" You lie !" interrupted Walter sternly. " You know that death will happen to him, even better than you know it will happen to me. But you wish not to be alone in your villany; you would bribe me into being your confederate, to keep silence, and to share your guilty gains. You are baser and viler even than I thought. To-morrow you will be known for what you are; but if you dare to tempt me any more, you shall be known to-day. There is some one coming this way; if you do not leave me, I swear I will tell him what you have done, be he who he may. Begone, I say!"

The approaching footsteps were now drawing very near, yet Sir Reginald still hesitated. "I have striven to save you, Walter Litton," he said hoarsely.

"Yes, to shame and infamy; I refuse to be saved upon such terms. It is hard to die, but I prefer the death that is awaiting me, to the life that awaits you, Reginald Selwyn."

As Walter pronounced the name in a loud voice, Sir Reginald pushed his straw hat over his eyes, and turned upon his heel, only just in time to avoid Francisco, who came up panting for breath. He had been running, which Walter had never known him to do before.

"Oh, Signor Litton, what is it that you are doing?"

"I am taking a walk on the Marina, Francisco," returned Walter, forcing a smile.

" But afterwards?"

"Well, afterwards, when I get to the wall yonder, I shall strike across into the country. Did you suppose I was going to throw myself into the sea?"

"No, signor; but you are about to do something as bad, or worse. Why have you left that money behind you, for me and Julia, as though we were never to see you more—and worse, for your own burial in the cemetery?"

"It is always best to provide against the worst, Francisco; then, whatever happens, the mind is calm. I did not know you would visit my room so quickly; but since you have done so, you may take the letters you have found there to their destinations: one to the English consul, and the other to Lady Selwyn."

"But none for her sister? Ah! that

alone gave me hope, for you would surely have written to the signora," said he, " had you intended never to return."

"Most certainly I should, my lad." Walter had enclosed his letter to Lilian in a note to Lotty, begging her not to deliver it until the former had regained her strength.

"Hush!" whispered Francisco. "Listen!"

From the trees which fringed the road upon the landward side there had come a sound which Walter understood only too well; Santoro was becoming impatient.

" Santa Rosalia! that is the brigand call, signor."

" I know it, Francisco; and I must needs obey it. Farewell! and Heaven be with you."

The next moment Walter had sprung over the wall and disappeared. Francisco uttered a cry of despair, and fled back at full speed towards the city.

CHAPTER XI.

THE PROMISE KEPT.

E must make good haste, signor," said Santoro, who was in waiting for Walter behind the wall. "That young fellow whom you have just parted from was the same who was watching us last evening at the cemetery. I am much mistaken if the troops are not sent out after us immediately, and it is possible that this time they may know where to find us."

He was referring of course to Corralli's camp, which, in that case, would have to shift its quarters, and the observation struck poor Walter as cool and selfish enough under the circumstances in which he was placed. He neither expected nor desired praise for the voluntary sacrifice of liberty and life that he was about to make, but that it should be thus altogether ignored, filled him with disgust. The fact was, however, that Santoro's intelligence was not sufficiently high to understand that the position of the young Englishman was altogether different from what that of one of his own fellow-countrymen would have been in similar straits. Had a Sicilian been suffered to escape Corralli's hands on similar conditions, he might also have fulfilled them—but upon compulsion; his wife, his children, his friends, would have all been held responsible for his breach of faith, and a terrible retribution would have been exacted from them. Yet even Santoro had a soft spot in his heart, as was presently made manifest. They had passed on their way for some time in silence, and having crossed the main road, were about to ascend the lower slopes of the mountain, when he thus addressed the companion who had once more become his prisoner: "I suppose, signor, you would never consent to become a brigand?"

"A brigand? Well, I have never considered the matter, Santoro, but I honestly tell you that I don't think it would suit me."

" Ah, the damp and the cold no doubt are unpleasant, and especially when there is not food enough to make one indifferent to them; still it is better to shiver a little, and even to want food and drink, than to die, signor."

" Doubtless, Santoro," answered Walter, unable to restrain a smile at his companion's simplicity and want of morals. " But there would be also other objections; and, besides, no one has offered me the alternative."

" Ah, but there is one who might do so. Look, signor, I have no desire to kill you, like some of those up yonder; on the contrary, I would have you live. You are brave, or you would not have smiled just now—you are strong and active; you would make as good a brigand as the best of us. Why not marry the signora ?"

" Marry the signora !" For the moment Walter did not understand to whom his companion was alluding, for there was but one woman to whom his thoughts reverted —she who in a few days would be mourning for his death, bereaved of love, almost ere love was born.

"Yes, marry the Signora Joanna. She adores you, Signor Litton, for Lavocca told me as much. Only consider the matter. We could both—that is, you and I—be married at the same time; then with our wives and the two other men we should form a separate band independent of that scoundrel Corbara, though of course we should be under orders as respects Corralli."

The crudity and childishness of this design were such as once more to try Walter's gravity, but he answered seriously enough: "My good friend, such a plan would be impossible under any circumstances."

"What! you would rather die than marry a pretty woman?"

"I did not say that; but I would certainly rather die than accept such conditions of existence as those you have proposed to me."

Santoro looked at his prisoner with amazement. "Well, you Englishmen are strange folks. I daresay you would not marry my Lavocca herself?"

" Indeed, if it were upon the same terms, I should be obliged to decline even that honour."

"Come on !" cried Santoro, with a gesture of impatience and disgust, as he started up the hill-side at the swing-trot peculiar to his class; nor did he utter another word for hours.

Walter was well aware that the proposition that had been made to him could never have originated with his companion, but had been most likely suggested to him by Larocca, who might certainly be supposed to know the inclinations of her mistress. On the other hand, he did not believe that the latter had authorized her to make it. Joanna, though ignorant and impulsive, had, he felt, an intelligence much too acute to entertain such an idea with seriousness. That she was in love with him, however, was certain, and in that love, he felt, lay his only hope—if hope there yet might be. She had already shown her good-will towards him, but in effecting what she had, had also shown the limits of her power. After a long climb in silence they came to an open space, the apex of a spur of the mountain, from which there was a magnificent view.

"By Heaven, there they are!" exclaimed Santoro suddenly.

Walter's heart beat fast as he heard him; he thought that they had already come within sight of those who were about to be his assassins. But the brigand's eyes were fixed upon the place from which they had ascended, on the main road, through which was passing a long column of troops; while in advance and to eastward of the hill on which they stood was a cloud of dust, with the sunlight glinting through it upon lance and helmet. It seemed to Walter as unreasonable that cavalry should be sent after them, as though a ship of war had been despatched on such a service, and he said so.

"Their object is," explained Santoro, "to surround us altogether before proceeding to attack the camp, the position of which it seems has been discovered. The Government is making a great effort for the English Milord, but it will not be to his advantage. If Corralli has caught sight of the soldiers, it is ten to one that it

will have gone hard with your friend
already."

" But surely he will have kept his word
with me as I with him; he gave us until
eight o'clock to-night."

For the moment it struck Walter that if
what Santoro said were true, and violence
had been already offered to the unhappy
merchant, he himself was under no obligation to keep his bargain; and what could be
easier than to run down the hill and join
the soldiers! The thought had hardly
crossed his brain, when the execution of it
was rendered impossible by the appearance
of two men with guns, who seemed to
spring out of the earth, and interposed
themselves between him and the road to
liberty. It was evident that they had been
lying in ambush, and that he had unconsciously passed by them on the way.
Of all faces that could meet his own at such
a time, those of these two men were the
most hateful and unwelcome, for the newcomers were Corbara and his creature
Canelli.

" Welcome, signor," said the former sar-
donically, and lifting his battered wide-

awake in mock salutation — " welcome,
though I see you come empty-handed. It
seems to me that you were half repenting of
having returned to us."

" Come, come, let us be fair," put in
Santoro good-naturedly; " the signor has
kept his word, and we have no right to
complain."

" No right to complain, when he has let
loose those dogs upon us !" and the speaker
pointed towards the soldiers. " They are
pouring in, it seems, from every point in
the compass; and yet, if they poured from
the sky itself, they would not save you, Mr.
Englishman."

" No, no ; they will not save him," echoed
Canelli grimly. " If they kill us, we will
have our fun first, lieutenant; will we
not ?"

" There, hark to the young bloodhound !"
continued Corbara, laughing. " He was not
so fortunate in winning the signora's money
from the rest of us as he expected to be,
and that has rather put him out. Has it
not ?"

" There are others, at all events, less in
luck than I am," answered the young

brigand, looking at Walter menacingly, and fingering the knife in his girdle. "They have not waited for eight o'clock with the old fellow up yonder, and why should we be more particular with this one?"

"Stand off!" cried Santoro sternly, "and keep your hands to yourself, or I will let daylight through you. I am answerable to the captain for my prisoner here, and you had better not interfere with him."

"Well, he will not give you much trouble after he gets up yonder," observed Corbara brutally; "only let us be all there before the play begins, remember; that's only fair." With that they parted, the two brigands moving down the hill, while Walter with his guard continued their ascent.

"Santoro," said he suddenly, "will you do me one favour before I die?

"Very readily, signor," answered the other, not without a touch of feeling in his tone. "What is it you would ask of me?"

"Only the loan of your knife."

"No, no; don't think of that yet, signor. If you will be guided by me, things may not be so bad with you even yet. It is always time enough to kill one's self."

"Not always, Santoro. Did you not hear what was just said to me?"

"Yes: but that fellow yonder is not everybody. Since you have come back like this, like a man of honour, and since, above all, Joanna loves you, you will not be tortured. She would never stand by and see it done."

"In that case, I shall not need your knife; but against the other chance, I entreat you to lend it me, Santoro."

"Will you promise not to use it against any of our own people—except Corbara? for if you have a fancy that way, I would not baulk it. I can believe your word, I know."

"Yes, Santoro; I promise."

"Then here is the knife."

Walter took it, and hid it in his breast. He had a surety now that death would be the worst that he could meet with. Hardly had he concealed the weapon, ere Colletta and another brigand emerged from the trees in front of them.

"Ha! you have come back then without the money!" cried Colletta the silent, looking at Walter with sullen disfavour.

"The signor is quite as sorry for that as

you can be," answered Santoro: " he has done his best, and failed."

"His best will be the worst for him," replied the other. " The captain is out of his mind with rage because of the troops being sent out again ; and since he never thought to see this young gentleman again, and, moreover, was indebted to him for their reappearance, he has been taking it out of the old one."

" Do you mean to say he has murdered my poor friend ?" ejaculated Walter with horror. He had heretofore tried to persuade himself that what Corbara had said about the merchant was a falsehood invented to give him pain.

" O dear no ; that would have been letting him off much too easily," answered Colletta coolly. " He only hung him up by one arm for an hour or so, with his toes touching the ground. The captain could hardly keep his knife out of the old scoundrel when he saw the troops instead of the ransom, and is gone down the mountain to cool himself by letting some blood."

" Then who is in command up yonder ?" inquired Santoro carelessly.

"The signora! There are not half a dozen altogether; Corralli has sent out the rest of us in pairs, to let the soldiers know that brigands have teeth."

The meaning glance which Santoro here cast at Walter fell upon barren ground; the young fellow's heart was full of pity for the unfortunate merchant, and it was one grain of solace to him at that moment to think that his reappearance would not be so bitter a disappointment to the captive as he had feared it would be. Mr. Brown must already be aware that all hopes of procuring the ransom were at an end.

The two brigands left them as their fellows had done, to take part in the bloodletting (of others), which Corralli had found necessary for his system or his temper; while Walter and his companion pushed on so quickly that before sunset, and therefore considerably in advance of the time appointed for their return, they presented themselves at the brigand camp. At the sight of them a murmur of sullen satisfaction broke forth from its inmates, very different from the extravagance of feeling commonly displayed among them ; and Joanna herself came forward to meet them with grave face.

" I ought not to say I am glad to see you, Signor Litton," said she in a low tone; " yet I can hardly be sorry that you have redeemed your word; I knew you would justify my confidence in it, though my brother scoffed at the idea, and has gone down yonder in the conviction that we should not see you."

" He was wrong, signora ; I am come back as I promised—to my death. All the favour I have to ask of him is, to let it be a quick one."

" Do not speak of that just yet, Signor Litton," answered she in a faltering voice ; " the time is not yet arrived."

" I know it ; and yet before that time, as your people have informed me, some cruelty has been perpetrated upon my unhappy friend, contrary to Corralli's promise."

" I could not help it," replied Joanna pleadingly ; " the sight of the troops put my brother beside himself with fury, and when he is here I am powerless."

" But when he is *not* here ?"

" Well, I can then do something, perhaps; and you may be sure," added she tenderly, " that all the power I have shall be at your service."

" I would wish then to speak with Mr. Brown at once."

A look of disappointment passed over Joanna's face; she had evidently anticipated some request upon his own account; but she bent her head in acquiescence, and Walter moved on without hindrance to the spot which his fellow-captive usually occupied. He found the old merchant sitting on the ground, and guarded by the two men who had joined the band with Joanna. As Walter drew nigh he lifted up a pale and haggard face, that showed such signs of pain as mental agony alone but rarely produces, and a sad smile lit up his features. " What! Walter, my lad, have you come back?" he murmured.

" Yes, my friend, did I not promise to do so?"

" Ah, yes; but I thought human nature would have been too strong for you. However, if they are not brute beasts, they will surely not treat you with such cruelty as they have treated me. I know now what it is to wish to die." A groan here escaped from the old man's heart that would have moved any heart save that of a brigand.

"They shall never torture you more," whispered Walter; "I have a knife here, which I am about to drop into your pocket. In the last extremity, you will know what to do with it."

"And you, Walter?" hesitated Mr. Brown, as he grasped the weapon.

"I shall take my chance. There are two hours yet before—before they will do us any hurt, unless Corralli should return. And while there is life there is hope."

The old man shook his head. "Nothing but a miracle could save us," answered he; "it is all over."

Walter had taken the precaution to bring with him a flask of brandy, and he now offered it to his companion, who put it greedily to his lips. The effect was instantaneous: the flame of life once more sprang up in its socket; and the familiar thoughts that had been numbed within him by despair were set free, and took their accustomed channel. "How is Lilian, Walter?"

"She is weak and wan, sir, but no longer suffering. She has been very, very ill, unhappily for us all; but I think she is on the road to health. She sent her dearest love, as Lady Selwyn did: but neither is as yet aware of our sad strait."

"That is well, since nothing can be done. Give me another drink, lad. How was it, Walter, that the payment of the ransom went amiss? Surely Gordon——"

"It was not Gordon, sir; it was Sir Reginald." And then in a few words he told him what had occurred.

The old merchant listened in silence, save for an interjection or two of indignation and abhorrence. "I had thought," said he quietly, when all was finished, " that there were no men in the world so wicked as these brigands, but it seems I was mistaken. Let us not sully our last thoughts by suffering them to dwell on such a villain."

But nevertheless he could not divert them from the topic, but again and again reproached himself with his own blindness to the baronet's true character, and always contrasting it with that of Walter. At any other time such comparisons would have been embarrassing, but the fact was Walter scarcely heard them, his own reflections, unstimulated by the fiery liquor which had made his companion garrulous, were running in a far deeper groove.

The sun had set, and it was near the hour which had been appointed as the limit of Walter's return, when he was roused from his meditations by Santoro.

"Signor Litton," said the brigand in low but earnest tones, "the signora would speak to you."

"Do not leave me, Walter!" exclaimed the old merchant piteously. "They are going to put us to death; but at least let us die together."

"Nothing will happen to either of you," said Santoro in answer to this appeal, the sense of which, if not the words, it was easy to understand, "until the captain returns."

"And then?" inquired Walter.

"Then you will die, and Milord here will begin to die."

Walter answered nothing, for he was sick at heart; but, with a face composed and calm, arose, and followed Santoro into Joanna's presence.

CHAPTER XII.

LEAP-YEAR.

I T was already dusk as Walter and Santoro crossed the camp, and where the few trees grew the light was so feeble that faces could scarcely be discerned ; it was more therefore by the short stature of Joanna than by her looks that Walter recognised the sister of the brigand chief, as she received him standing in the shadow of some beech-trees. Santoro, in obedience to a gesture from his mistress, had at once withdrawn, and they were quite alone.

"I have sent for you, Signor Litton," said she in a strange and trembling voice, "to say what it does not become a woman's lips to say, though it delights her ear to listen to it. The peril in which you stand, the imminence of it, and—and—something in my own heart must plead as my excuse : I love you !"

The fact was not certainly unknown to Walter; but the confession of it, made thus abruptly, and under such abnormal circumstances, astounded him—perhaps with that " amazement" with which our English marriage service credits young persons of the opposite sex. Having heard thus much, he did not doubt that the proposition hinted at by Santoro—that he should save his life by wedding Joanna, while at the same time adopting her profession—was about to be made to him.

" Joanna——" he began.

" Pray let me finish ere you answer me," interrupted she, in the same trembling tones, but with an earnest pleading in them that gave them force. " It cannot be but that you scorn me at the outset, but I can bear your scorn, since it is for your own sake that I provoke it. From the first instant that I saw you, I became your prisoner, though you were mine; my woman's heart acknowledged you its lord; the courage you have shown, the honour you have exhibited,

15

it took for granted without trial. I should have known them had I died that moment, as well as now when they have been proved so gallantly and at so great a sacrifice. When I showed you the secret of our cavern, and bade you depart if it so pleased you, it was but a girl's artifice to show her trust, for I felt that I ran no risk of losing you that way; and later, when I became as it were bail for your returning hither, though it pained me to see you go, I knew you would return and redeem your promise, as certainly as I know it to-day. O, signor, what was it but love that told me so! Here, in my bosom, I keep the picture that you drew of my poor self; but nearer yet and within my heart is your own image, and will remain there to my dying day, though that indeed will be soon if you die. Oh, why"—here her voice grew passionately earnest, though her tone was little above a whisper—"should we speak of death, we two, when it can be averted from us both!"

"I see not how, Joanna," answered Walter gravely.

"Ah, but I can show you how. For your sake, I am content to give up—it is not much you will say, but it is all I have—my place among my people, and its power; to exchange this free air and untrammelled life, for an existence that must needs seem cramped and submissive; my native land for yours; if only you will let me call you mine! Oh, do not scorn such love!"

She stopped for an instant, overcome with emotion, and Walter said: "I do not scorn it, Joanna."

"I thank you, signor, even for that much of kindness," continued she submissively. "I pray you hear me out. Corralli, look you, though he is black in your eyes, is my brother, dear to me as the only kin I have, and one who has avenged my wrongs; yet to wed you I will desert him, returning evil for good. I have no bent for this dishonest life; my hand is free from blood, and it is yours if you will but please to accept it. I cannot flatter myself, alas! that you would do so, if you were free to choose, but since it holds your life in it, signor, my poor love may help to make it worth your taking."

During the latter part of Joanna's appeal,

the passionate eloquence with which she had at one time urged it had quite failed her, though the plaintive tenderness still lingered. Doubtless she read in Walter's face not only that her love was unreturned, but that it could never be so. Or perhaps the humiliation of having to offer so huge a bribe, for what she would have fain obtained without the asking, quenched all her natural fire. This despondent pleading, however, by no means lost her ground with him to whom it was addressed. Walter had, it is true, no love to give her; but he had pity, which is said to be akin to it; and gratitude, which tends towards it; while, above all, the natural desire for life—life almost at any price—was pulling at his heart-strings. If he should promise to wed Joanna, he would hardly be forsworn, since to the girl he would have wed he was already dead—or would be so in a few hours; marriage with Lilian was an impossibility; then why not save his life by marriage with Joanna? Men marry every day without affection, to gain much less; nor in his case—a mere Bohemian without kith or kin—were the social objections to such a union—

stupendous as they would have been with some men—by any means insurmountable. The only member of society who was likely to have any voice in the matter—namely, Jack Pelter—would probably hail with enthusiasm the addition of a female brigand chief to their *ménage* in Beech Street; or regard her at worst as a gratis model of the Salvator Rosa class, and an admirable addition to the establishment. These thoughts, practical and even humorous, flashed upon Walter's brain, in spite of himself, though death was hovering over him, and genuine if misdirected love was demanding a final answer to its appeal. But they came and went in a second of time, and left him calm and steadfast. As to purchasing his personal safety at this price, or any price, that, had it stood alone, would have been his own affair, to be settled with his own conscience. He was not so quixotic as to hold Lilian's love as plighted troth, when death itself had put in, as it were, a priority of claim to him; in any case he could not be Lilian's, and therefore it was unreasonable that he should accuse himself of faithlessness in wedding another. But there was a feature in this case which made it easy indeed for him to come to a just decision. How was it possible for him to return to Palermo a free man with such news as he would have to bring with him? Could he tell Lilian that he had saved his life on the condition of marrying Joanna, but had left her father to perish by unheard-of tortures at the hands of men made still more furious by his own escape? Would not the twofold woe be her death-doom, and the life he had thus basely purchased for himself become intolerable from shame, as that of Sir Reginald himself. He had not the shadow of a doubt of it, and therefore no hesitation as to what it became him to reply.

"Joanna," said he, "so far from scorning the love which you offer me at so great a sacrifice to yourself, I am deeply sensible of it, and thank you for it with all my heart; but the last words spoken by yonder unhappy man: 'Do not leave me, Walter,' and which are still ringing in my ears, have greater force than even those which promise me life and liberty. I cannot accept these gifts, for they would be worthless to me since they would have been purchased by the desertion of my friend."

For a full minute Joanna was silent; then she took a step towards him, and laid her hand upon his shoulder. "Walter," she said, "rather than lose you I will save your friend. It will be difficult, and very dangerous, but I will do my best to do it. I had promised to desert my brother, though you will not desert this man, who is not even of your blood; but I will do yet more —I will play Corralli false, and rob him of what he holds to be his just revenge. For your sake, and to win you for my own, I will become a traitress. This very night—nay, within this very hour, for we have no time to lose—I will place you both in safety, if you will pass your word to be my husband. Oh, what can woman's love give more. Hark!"

Through the stillness of the night was heard the firing of musket-shots at a great distance. "Yonder Corralli speaks. He will be up here shortly, wild with rage and loss. No power of mine will then avail to save you. Quick, quick! give me your Word."

Again a torrent of contending thoughts swept through Walter's brain. The circumstances in which he was now placed had become strangely altered. If Joanna could carry out her present offer, Lilian would lose indeed her lover (though not, alas, his love), but she would at least have left to her her father. It would be no longer for his own sake, but for hers that he would become another's. His hand he could not offer her, but in its place he would give her her father's life.

Again was heard a dropping fire of musketry, but the sound was more distinct. The combatants were evidently coming nearer.

"Walter, your hand!" whispered Joanna eagerly; "in a few minutes more it may be too late."

"I give it you, Joanna. If you will save the old man's life, I promise to make you my wife."

Never surely was betrothal made under circumstances so ill-assorted and inapt; nor was there one moment to spare for its tender ratification.

"Santoro, Colletta," cried Joanna in loud

and commanding tones, "let both the prisoners be fast secured."

This was done at once with ropes that bit into their arms; and helpless as infants Walter and Mr. Brown were placed side by side upon the ground. The brigands crowded round them with wrathful and excited looks, which the noise of the firing had doubtless evoked; they imagined that vengeance was already to be taken upon their wretched captives.

"Corralli is beset down yonder," exclaimed Joanna, "and we must send him succour. Now these men are bound, we women are their masters, and can be left to guard them. Let each take his musket and do his part; and when it is done, you will find us here in charge."

There was an instant of hesitation, but used to the habit of obedience, the men moved to where the arms were piled, and each one took his weapon. Santoro alone remained standing beside the women.

"Get you gone, Santoro; it is you who will be in command till you join my brother," said Joanna imperiously.

"No, signora; I remain here at all

hazards," answered he in low significant tones.

"You disobey then my express orders?"

"For the present, signora, yes. I venture to think the captain would wish the prisoners to be left with a stronger guard than yourself and Lavocca."

"If you remain, you will do so at your peril."

"That I quite understand, signora. Corralli will decide when he comes up the hill again as to which of us was in the right."

By this time the band were ready to march, and, in their presence, all controversy was to one, at least, of the disputants out of the question.

"You will obey Colletta, men, till you fall in with the captain," said Joanna steadily; "upon second thoughts, I will keep Santoro to guard the camp."

"Good!" exclaimed Colletta, who was well content to find himself in the unwonted position of commander. "There is no knowing what prisoners may not be up to. Now then, my fine fellows, step out." And off started the brigands at their

" double," which was a run about twice as fast as that used by regular soldiers, and of course without the least pretence of order, which indeed the nature of the ground would itself have rendered impossible. Santoro watched them disappear, then with a grim smile turned round upon Joanna : " It was well schemed, signora ; but I am not quite such a fool as Lavocca has doubtless represented me to be."

" On the contrary, Lavocca has always spoken well of you in that respect. 'You have plenty of wits,' she says, 'but, unfortunately, no heart.'"

" No heart ! I, who love her with all my soul, and would lay down my life for her !"

" Oh, she has heard you say that, doubtless, perhaps a thousand times. But when it comes to the proof of your affection, then it is that you are found wanting."

" Begging your pardon, signora," answered the brigand, reddening, " and with all due submission to you as Corralli's sister, you are speaking what is not the truth."

" You talk of submission, and yet you

remain here in defiance of my orders!" returned Joanna contemptuously. "You talk of love, and yet it was Lavocca's wish, as well as my own, that we should be left alone here!"

"Ay; to let those birds yonder out of the cage, or at all events the one that, to your ear, seems to sing so sweetly. You would doubtless find your own account in such a plan, signora; but what advantage would it be to Lavocca, who would only share the transgression and the punishment?"

"It is love then, and not duty, that keeps you here, Santoro?"

"It is both, signora," answered the brigand, smiling, for at a sign from her mistress her companion drew near, whose presence to his rugged nature was as the sun that draws from a barren soil unlooked-for signs of graciousness and fertility: "it is duty to yourself, and love for Lavocca."

"Then what I have now to ask of you, Santoro, will be easy to grant," continued Joanna. "It is my intention to set loose these captives, and lead them to Palermo. You may oppose it, of course, but it will be at the loss of one of our two lives ; and if you should kill me, you will not find it easy, I think, to win Lavocca——"

"I would not marry him if he did, though there was not another man in the world," interposed Lavocca resolutely; "I would even rather marry Corbara."

"She would marry Corbara!" exclaimed Santoro, lifting up his hands, as if in appeal to universal nature against an idea so monstrous.

"But on the other hand," continued Joanna, "if you will come into our plans, and assist us to escape, Lavocca will marry you as soon as we set foot in the city. A free pardon will easily be obtained for us in consideration of this service to the Englishmen——"

"And your brother would flay us alive before the week was out," interrupted Santoro.

"If he caught us; I don't doubt that in the least," answered Joanna. "But Milord yonder will place you on board his yacht, and you will never leave it until you and your wife are landed in England, where he will provide for you handsomely. Of course there will be danger in getting down the mountain, but if you will not run some risk to win Lavocca, you, who were talking about laying down your life for her——"

She did not finish the sentence, because Lavocca had with the most opportune judgment precipitated herself into her lover's arms, and he was covering her comely face with kisses : the noise they made, however, was so very slight that Joanna felt justified in taking it for the silence that gives consent. "Come, come," said she; "you will have leisure enough for that to-morrow. You must earn your reward, Santoro, before enjoying it!" Yet nevertheless she left the fond pair together while she flew across the camp, and with a sharp knife cut the ropes that bound the prisoners, at the same time whispering a few words into Walter's ear.

"Is it then come at last?" cried the old merchant feebly : "is death awaiting us ?"

"No ; life and freedom, if you have only the courage to take advantage of the opportunity," replied Walter. In the excitement of the moment he had almost forgotten the price he had agreed to pay for them, and he bounded to his feet like a deer. " Give me a weapon, Joanna."

She drew a pistol from her belt, and gave it him. " Santoro yonder is on our side, dearest, and will lead us down the mountain. If we part again, it will not be your death alone that will separate us, but mine also."

He answered, not with the caress which perhaps she expected, but with a silent pressure of his hand.

CHAPTER XIII.

THE ESCAPE.

N a few minutes the whole party had left the camp, and plunged into the shadow of the trees that thickly covered the mountain, and which at that hour as effectually concealed them as though the earth had swallowed them up. The foliage, however, was intermittent; large spaces of exposed ground had presently to be crossed, where the dusk of a Sicilian night afforded them but a scanty cloak; and when this happened, Santoro and the two women walked in advance, that their dress might deceive the eyes of their late comrades, and cause them to be taken for a portion of the band under Colletta. They were only too likely to fall in with some of these, since it was the brigand habit when

entering into action, to scatter in pairs;
though, on the other hand, this might
enable the fugitives to overcome opposition.
Having once embraced their cause and his
Lavocca, Santoro could be depended upon
to fight for them, and indeed he had gone
too far to render return to his original
allegiance possible. His untiring step fell
as noiselessly upon the rock as on the turf,
his keen eyes roved from tree to tree with
unceasing vigilance, and though the night
was cloudy and their way without a path, he
never lost the true direction of their course;
only, when shots were heard, he would stop
and listen, and turn to the right hand or
the left in order to avoid the combatants,
from whose neighbourhood they were still,
however, at a considerable distance. Three
out of his four companions, albeit two were
women, took step for step with his own;
but for the fourth—Mr. Christopher Brown
—the whole party had not seldom to halt
while he panted for breath, or begged for a
drop of water to quench his thirst. His
age and constitution were but ill fitted for a
night-march of such speed and duration,
and, moreover, the terrors and privations

of the previous fortnight had much enfeebled his frame. In his own mind, Walter felt but too sure that in case of their having to fight their way, the poor merchant must needs succumb to adverse fate, and would never survive to enjoy that liberty which he had so loyally striven to procure for him.

They had descended about two-thirds of the mountain, and consequently had reached what was the most dangerous part of the journey—namely, the locality where in all probability, the brigands' line intervened between them and the troops, when suddenly "the call" was heard very soft and low immediately in front of them. Walter and Mr. Brown, who were just issuing from a copse into an open space, at once stepped back among the trees; but the three others, who had advanced farther, and whose appearance had doubtless evoked the signal, moved boldly on, Santoro, with admirable presence of mind, at the same time giving back the answering note. The next moment they were confronted by Corbara. Of all the band, next to Corralli himself, this man was the most to be dreaded; for not only

was he a most determined and relentless
ruffian, and possessed of vast physical
strength, but he was especially hostile to
Santoro. On the other hand, he was probably unaware of the succour sent by Joanna,
and would therefore not be so suspicious of
her presence as if he had known she had
been left in charge of the prisoners; and
what was also hopeful was that he appeared
to be alone. Santoro, who had already
loosened his pistols in his belt, would have
shot him down at once, but for fear that he
might have comrades near him, and the
most bitter repentance that he had ever experienced seized his soul because he had
parted with his knife to Walter.

"Ah! Santoro, how comes it that you
are down here?—and La Signora also!"
Here he stepped back with a movement of
suspicion. "What has caused you to leave
the camp?"

"We are come to help my brother,"
answered Joanna coolly; "the firing came
so quick that I felt he must be hardly
pressed."

"He is only fighting because he likes it,"
answered Corbara gruffly; "for my part, it

seems to me that there is blood enough to be spilt for the present, without losing our own in return."

This was a reference, as Joanna well understood, to the promised fate of the captives, and in her ignorance as to whether they were not even at that moment within sight of the speaker, she felt that her presence of mind was being tried to the uttermost; fortunately, her nerves were like her muscles, strong as steel.

"I hope there has been no loss amongst us?" inquired she earnestly.

"As to loss of life, I know not, though when there are bullets singing about our ears as plentifully as birds in June, it is more than likely; but I for one have lost blood enough."

"Well, here is she who will bind up your wound, Corbara, and give you more comfort than the best surgeon in Palermo," and Joanna signed to Lavocca to approach the lieutenant. As she did so, Santoro whispered: "Your knife, your knife!" and the young girl slipped it into his hand as she moved past him towards his rival.

"It is but a scratch in the right shoulder,

my dear," said Corbara, in a tone which he
intended to be tender; "and if you have
got a handkerchief—— What's that?" A
piercing cry broke from the covert from
which they had just emerged, and almost at
the same moment a groan from Corbara,
who staggered and fell forward on his face ;
a blow from Santoro's knife, struck between
the shoulders, had cloven his heart in
twain.

"Hark, hark !" cried Joanna; "there is
mischief behind us ; see to Signor Litton."
She was herself the first to reach the spot
where she had left Walter and his companion, and where were now three persons.
The youth Colletta lay on the ground, felled
by the butt of Walter's pistol, though not
before he had uttered a cry for help, which
was already answered to left and right of
them ; they could even hear the noise of
men forcing their way towards them through
the brushwood.

" Quick, quick !" cried Santoro ; " straight
down the hill every one of you." And all
five ran forward together, though it seemed
that such a movement must cast them into
the very arms of their foes. Again and

again a sheet of flame flashed out upon
them, and one at least of their number
toppled over. It was not Mr. Brown,
Walter knew, for he was holding the old
man firmly by the arm, and helping him
on, as a father helps his child to keep up
with his longer legs; and it was not
Joanna, for she never left his side, and at
each flash seemed as though she would have
interposed her own lithe form between himself and the bullet. Thus they held on their
headlong way for a considerable time, when
the old merchant suddenly fell exhausted on
the ground, with the last breath he had to
spare bidding Walter leave him to his fate,
since another yard he could not run. Then
for the first time they missed Santoro. The
noise of the firing had ceased; there were
no signs of their pursuers; and the grey
dawn was slowly breaking over the eastern
hills. Yet self-congratulation was by no
means the prevailing feeling with their little
band.

" Where is he ?" cried Lavocca wildly.
" He was close behind me all the way, and
again and again bade me be of good courage.
If he has fallen into their hands, I will

avenge him yet"—and the determined girl
had actually begun to reascend the mountain when Joanna seized her arm.

" He is not in their hands, Lavocca, but
with the saints, I trust," whispered she
tenderly; " I saw him leap into the air ten
minutes back, killed by a bullet through his
brain."

" You saw him die, and yet you ran on?
Oh, cruel, cruel!" cried the unhappy girl.

" What aid could we have given him,
dear Lavocca? Would you have had us
make the triumph of his murderers still
greater by becoming their prisoners? His
dearest wish, if he could now express it,
would be that you should effect your escape.
Let us now think only of obeying him, and
mourn him afterwards."

Accustomed to submit in everything to
Joanna's will, Lavocca was to all appearance
herself again before they resumed their
flight; she shed no more tears, but instead
of using her former vigilance, kept her eyes
fixed on the ground, as though she cared
little now what fortune happened to her,
and lagged somewhat behind the rest. It
was a harsh blow of fate that had deprived

her of the being who was so soon to have
been her husband, but, as a matter of fact,
she had been by no means passionately
devoted to poor Santoro; the love, as in her
mistress's case, had been almost wholly on
one side, only in the reverse order as to sex;
and, moreover, Lavocca was a coquette in
her way, with no stronger feeling of any
kind than that of exciting admiration.
Joanna indeed was as much grieved as she
at their late companion's death, for she
could not but be aware that she herself had
been the involuntary cause of it. But, on
the other hand, now that the pursuit of
those whom she had such good cause to fear
was over, or seemed to be so, and while the
reward for which she had fought so hard
seemed within her grasp, her heart had
scarce room for grief. The dawn had
broadened into daylight, and from where
they stood, upon a low spur of the mountain, some portion of their city of refuge
was to be seen. "See, Walter," whispered
she triumphantly, as they moved side by
side together: "yonder is Palermo; the
troops are not far from hence; but in any
case, in one hour more, you will be free,

and I shall be bound only by the sweet ties of love and duty."

The words had scarce escaped her lips, when a line of fire, accompanied by a splutter of musketry broke out from a small thicket close to the right of them, and she dropped down at his feet like a stone. When the blinding bitter smoke had rolled away, Walter, kneeling by her prostrate form, found himself surrounded by a crowd of soldiers, astonished to see the young Englishman moved to tears by the just retribution that had overtaken one of his captors. Lavocca, whom they took for a boy brigand, was bound hand and foot; and Mr. Christopher Brown was drinking brandy as though it were water from a flask which the officer in command was holding to his lips.

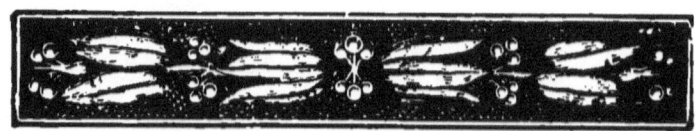

CHAPTER XIV.

JOANNA was not dead; but she had received more than one wound, which the surgeon of the detachment pronounced to be very serious. As soon as they were bound up and she could be moved, a litter was brought, in which she was conveyed slowly towards the town; and beside it walked Walter and Lavocca. A brief explanation of the matter had of course been given by the former, and the two women at once divided the interest of their captors with those whom they had been sent out to rescue. Poor Mr. Brown, indeed, as he limped along all draggled and torn, with anything but that smooth starched look which distinguishes the rich citizens of London, was by no means an

attractive object; but since his pecuniary
value was well understood, he did not lack
attention.   Altogether the procession was a
sombre one, very unlike what the return of
an expedition should be which has accomplished its object.   For the soldiers were
aware that they had not only " encumbered
with their assistance" the persons whom
they had gone out to succour, but had inflicted a grievous wrong on her to whom
the escape of the prisoners had been owing ;
while Mr. Brown was too exhausted, and
Walter too overcome with pity for his pre-
server, to show any symptom of satisfaction.
As she was lifted speechless into the litter,
she had feebly held out her hand to him,
and he had carried it to his lips, and
retained it still.   The soldiers thought that
the young Englishman was but expressing
his gratitude by so doing; but he would
have done the same had it been an open
sign of their engagement.   He was too full
of commiseration and thankfulness to her,
to abate one jot of an exhibition of affection
which evidently gave her an intense
pleasure ; nor, whatever his unbidden
thoughts might have been, did he permit

himself to speculate upon what fortune might have in store for him should her wounds prove mortal. His whole existence was for the time devoted to her; the remembrance of his former life, including even his late experiences while in Corralli's power, were all swept away, to make room as it were for the absorbing reflection that this girl had given to him her love, and had proved its genuineness by sacrificing for him all she had—even perhaps to life itself.

At a small village on their way a mule was found, whereon Mr. Brown was lifted, which enabled him to converse as well as keep pace with his late companion.

"Walter Litton, you are henceforth my son, remember, whatever happens," were his first words, spoken with great feeling. "I mean," added he, as the young painter stared at him half dazed with woe and wonder, "whatever happens as respects dear Lilian."

How strange it seemed that such a communication should give him pain; but yet it did so. He only bowed his head, by way of acknowledgment; then turned to Joanna in terror lest she should have understood

the old man's words. Whether they referred to Lilian's state of health or her
feelings towards himself (of which he had
never spoken openly to her father), he did
not know, but it brought her home to his
remembrance, and in so doing seemed to do
a wrong to his wounded charge.

" This young woman, to whom we owe
so much," continued Mr. Brown, misunder-
standing his glance, " will of course be
taken to our hotel, to be tended by my
daughters like a sister."

" Indeed she deserves no less, sir,"
answered Walter solemnly.

Nothing more was said until they drew
near the city, when Mr. Brown once more
broke silence: " I wonder whether that
scoundrel Selwyn will venture to look me
in the face?" The old merchant's mental
vigour was evidently returning to him now
that he had reached the confines of civiliza-
tion; while Walter, who had been the
leading spirit throughout their common
dangers, felt on the contrary more perplexed
and subdued with every footfall. Notwithstanding the earliness of the hour, a great
crowd, upon whom Joanna's dark eyes

rested without seeming to observe their presence, accompanied the procession to the hotel, where the good news had already penetrated, and on the steps of which stood the landlord, to do honour to their arrival.

"Is Sir Reginald Selwyn within?" was Mr. Brown's impatient inquiry, delivered in very disinheritory tones.

"No, sir; he left yesterday by the steamer to Messina. Her ladyship, your daughter, however, did not accompany him."

In another minute, ere he reached the head of the stairs, the old man was clasped in Lotty's arms. To his astonishment, and still more to that of Walter, Lilian herself, pale and trembling, and looking like one risen from the grave, was standing at the doorway of the sitting-room. But ere she could shape the words of welcome, her eyes fell upon the litter, as it was slowly borne upstairs, and concluding doubtless that it contained Walter, sick or wounded, her feeble strength forsook her, and she would have fallen senseless on the floor, but for her father's aid. He kissed her tenderly; and then, still hugging her to his breast, observed to Lotty: "You will have two patients to nurse now, my girl, instead of one. This is a woman—though you wouldn't think so," continued he, pointing to Joanna —"and one to whom Walter and myself are indebted for our lives. And here is another young person in male attire. We have been in very queer company of late, as you will conclude; but these two are by far the best specimens of it, I do assure you."

It was quite curious to see how quickly the old merchant had recovered from his late depression, and how naturally he reassumed the position of host and master, which he had occupied before his late misfortunes. Poor Lavocca, on the other hand, bereft of her lover, alarmed for the fate of her only friend, and overcome by the strangeness of the scene, so different from those of her mountain-life, looked piteous and disconsolate enough, and kissed the hand which Lotty held out to her with grateful humility.

"Now, Walter, my lad," continued Mr. Brown, "you had better go home and make yourself comfortable, while I do the like,

and then come up here to breakfast, and
hear the doctor's report. I have sent for
the best in the place; and if money can
save her, Miss Joanna shall not want for
life, or anything that life can give her."

Walter would have hesitated to obey this
order, for he felt that his place was by the
side of the wounded girl, whom he had
promised to make his wife; but the arrival
of the surgeon, who instantly ordered the
patient to be conveyed into the inner room,
and the apartment to be cleared, put the
matter beyond his power, and compelled
him to retire to his lodgings. Here he
remained in a strange state of anxiety and
suspense, scarcely knowing what to hope or
what to fear; now moved with tender pity
for Joanna, now filled with still more tender
regrets upon Lilian's account; and very ill
inclined to listen to the congratulations with
which Baccari and his son overwhelmed
him, but which gratitude compelled him to
acknowledge. For it was indeed to the
interest which Francisco had taken in him,
and the promptness with which he had
acted, upon seeing him depart with Santoro,
that his rescue had been due. The lad had

entertained some suspicion of his not being
a free agent, during those last days he had
spent in Palermo, and had watched his
proceedings accordingly; had dogged him
to the gate of the cemetery, and contrived
to overhear the name of the locality where
Corralli had pitched his camp. Then, when
convinced of the young Englishman's departure and its object, he had hurried to
the consul with the letter Walter had left
behind him, and had also delivered that for
Lilian into the hands of his mistress, her
attendant. In consequence of these rapid
measures, the troops had been sent out
forthwith, with better information than
usual as to the direction in which to march,
and with orders to surround the mountain.
The impatience and fury of Corralli himself
had done the rest. But besides sending out
the troops, the tidings thus disseminated by
Francisco had roused public indignation,
not only among the British residents, but
with the natives themselves, against Sir
Reginald; and it was amid a storm of hisses
and execrations that he had embarked on
board the steamer on the previous afternoon.
He had not indeed been driven to do so by

the general indignation ; his natural courage
would probably have been too high for that;
but after having witnessed Walter's departure, he had felt inaction insupportable.
To stay in Palermo and await the news
of the massacre that he could have prevented by the mere signing of his name,
was something that even his iron nerves
refused to face ; and therefore he had taken
his place for Messina. He would willingly
have carried Lotty with him, since, in her
despair and wretchedness at the coming
catastrophe, she was only too likely to
drop some hint that would lead to his
inculpation ; but, on the other hand, to tear
her away at such a time from her sick
sister, was an act which would set every
tongue wagging against him, and still more
certainly arouse suspicion. So Sir Reginald
had gone alone, to the great relief of all concerned, save the mob, who wished to duck
him, and Mr. Brown, who—no longer restrained by sentiments of respect for the
baronet of the United Kingdom—yearned to
give him large pieces of his mind.

In the midst of these details came a
message from the hotel, to say that Walter's

presence was required there at once; he hurried thither, and found Lotty awaiting him in the sitting-room alone.

" I don't understand the matter at all, Mr. Litton," said she nervously. " Everything has been so strange and terrible, that it may well have done away with my poor wits; but this poor brigand woman, it seems, is dying; and though Lilian is most unfit to be her companion under such circumstances, she has insisted upon being with her, and now you have been sent for to see them both—alone."

Walter's heart was too full to speak; he only bowed, and followed Lotty through the door that led into the sick-room. She ushered him within it, and then immediately withdrew, taking Julia and Lavocca with her; and Walter found himself alone with the two women, to each of whom—but out of devotion to one of them—he had plighted his troth. Joanna, looking strangely unlike herself in feminine garb, and with features from which the near approach of death had chased every touch of harshness, and left all womanly, was lying on Lilian's couch; while Lilian—with cheeks as pale as those of

17—2

her companion, and which she in vain strove
to keep free from tears—was sitting in an
armchair by her side.   She signed to him
in silence to draw near Joanna.

"I have sent for you, Signor Litton,"
began the latter in weak and broken tones ;
when a gentle hand was suddenly placed
upon her arm, and a soft voice interrupted
her with : " Why not call him Walter !"
" Ah, you have a good heart," murmured
the dying girl.   " Yes, I will call him
Walter, since it is for so short a time.
Walter, I have sent for you to bid you farewell.   The doctor tells me—though indeed
I felt that it was so before he came—that I
am dying.   It is better that this should be,
even on my own account, for what had I to
live for save a love that could never be
returned ; and upon yours, how much
better, since it will set you free."

Walter's eyes were fixed upon her with
an ineffable tenderness and pity as he
replied : " Do you suppose then that I wish
you to die, Joanna, *you* who have just
preserved my life ?"

" No ; you are too generous, too unselfish,
to wish that; but, nevertheless, my death

will make you happy, and therefore death is welcome to me. It was but a mad dream of mine—but I am a poor ignorant foolish girl—that I could ever win your love. I see that now. Yet you won mine, all that I had to give, Walter, and you will keep it still; it is not like this other one's" (here she smiled on Lilian), "yet something not altogether worthless to think of now and then, and draw a sigh from you. I hope that I shall not be quite forgotten, Walter?"

"You will never be forgotten, Joanna, while the life that you have given still abides within me."

"And if I had lived you would have kept your word?"

"I would have made you my wife, so help me, Heaven!"

"Brave heart, brave heart!" continued Joanna. "He tells the truth to man and woman. You knew this before, Lilian, but he did not know you knew. Give me your hand, Walter. This hand is mine," she murmured, carrying it to her parched lips, "and I have the right to dispose of it. Now, Lilian, give me yours." Then she

took Lilian's hand and placed it in Walter's.
"You are worthy of him; you will make
him happy, as I never could have done.
May Heaven bless you both!"

The physical exertion she had used had
been very slight, yet she seemed greatly
exhausted.

"Indeed, Joanna, you must say no more,"
whispered Lilian caressing her. "Walter
must go away for the present; you are
doing yourself harm."

"As you please," murmured Joanna with
a sad smile, "though I do not think I can
take harm. But before he goes—he is
yours now, Lilian; I have made him over
to you—may I ask of him to kiss me?"

Walter bent low, half blind with tears,
and gave Joanna his first kiss: it was his
last one also, for she died within an hour or
so, quite suddenly, in Lotty's arms, whom
she took for Lilian, whose scanty strength
had succumbed to the late excitement.

"Be good to him, dear," were the poor
girl's last words. "He is worth all love
can give him."

CHAPTER XV.

HOMEWARD BOUND.

OR a few days after the return of the captives, it seemed probable that Walter would have lost not only his plighted bride, but her also to whose loving arms she had bequeathed him. The knowledge of her father's sufferings in the brigand camp, and of the fate which he had so narrowly escaped; her rival's death; and the disclosure of Reginald's perfidy, had so tried Lilian's feeble frame, that it almost lost its foothold upon existence. For weeks she lay, prostrated as before, and only able to see Walter for a few minutes; and it was well-nigh winter before she could get about, and, leaning on his arm, face the mild rigours of the Sicilian air. In the meantime he was, of course, thrown much

into the society of Mr. Brown, who seemed
as though he could never sufficiently show
his contrition for having so unjustly banished
him from it upon that memorable evening
at Willowbank. The merchant had recovered his old ways and habits of command
with miraculous elasticity with respect to
other people, but to Walter he never failed
to exhibit a deferential as well as an affec-
tionate regard. It was, however, expressed
in a characteristic way; not demonstratively
as to words and manner, but in a sober
practical fashion, such as became a pillar of
commerce. "I had never believed," said he
one evening, as they were smoking together
on the veranda of the hotel, "that the phrase,
'His word is as good as his bond,' could be
taken in a literal sense; but you indeed
have proved it to be so. That you should
have come back again from all this life and
liberty" — he pointed to the swarming
Marina, and the sparkling bay that bordered
it, flecked with many a sail—"to death and
torture, just because you had given your
promise to do so, without an inch of stamped
paper, is a very fine thing, my lad. I had
come to know you better by that time; but

yet I never thought so well of you as to believe you would have returned empty-handed to that den of thieves."

"Well, as to my word being as good as my bond, Mr. Brown," answered Walter, laughing, "that is not so great a compliment as it seems. for I fancy my bond would not be worth much."

"It would be good for fifty thousand pounds, my man," observed the merchant gravely.

"How so, Mr. Brown?"

"Because that is the sum I am going to give you and Lilian for your marriage present. Why not, sir? If I had escaped Corralli's hands by any other means save those you contrived for me, I should have paid the money into the brigand treasury; and surely one may at least prefer to put it in the pocket of an honest young English-man. Then the saving my life may be reckoned as some value received, I suppose; not to mention my daughter's life, which, had I been put to death, would, I verily believe, have been sacrificed. Moreover, I am under an immense obligation to you for unmasking that scoundrel, Sir Reginald.

What a pretty existence he would have led poor Lotty, and how all my hard-earned gains would have been frittered away on the racecourse or the gambling-table, if it had not been for you, my lad! No, no; I wont have a word of thanks, for the obligation will still be upon my own side, after all is done. Pooh, pooh! The money shall be settled upon Lilian and her children, then, if you wish it to be so; though there will be plenty more for them, I daresay. What's hers will be yours, you know, and being a prudent young fellow, I daresay you'll find the income sufficient." And Mr. Christopher Brown chuckled, as at one time, not so long ago, and in a certain locality, now white with snow, which he could almost catch sight of from where they were sitting, he had hardly thought to chuckle again.

"Have you heard anything more of Sir Reginald lately, sir?" inquired Walter, after some more talk to the same effect, in which the baronet's name had again been mentioned.

"Yes; I have had a telegram from his lawyer, enclosed from Naples, this very day: '*My client accepts the terms proposed to him,*

and will give the undertaking required.' Of
course he will. So long as he gets his
thousand a year, paid quarterly, he will be
content to remain separated from his be-
loved wife. She will be free enough from
any molestation from him, you may depend
upon it."

Walter nodded, and sighed: he was
thinking of the old times when Reginald
Selwyn had been a hero in his eyes at school
and college. Had he been base from the
beginning? he wondered. Was it a false
glitter that had dazzled all eyes concerning
him, or had his nature deteriorated from
circumstances? Had want of money made
him value it too highly? and when fortune
seemed to be within his grasp, had he been
unable to resist the temptation to snatch at
it? He had been always selfish, and somewhat hard, but surely not so heartless and
cruel as these last days had proved him to
be. Nor could Walter forget the impulse
of old friendship that had caused the
wretched man to follow him along the
Marina yonder, as he went to his doom,
and strive to save him from it—though only
by making him partaker of his crime.

"I am afraid," sighed he, "Lotty will not receive this news with the same satisfaction as yourself, Mr. Brown. After all, this man was her first-love."

"First fiddlesticks!" exclaimed the old merchant impatiently. "You would try to persuade me that my daughter is a fool, to my face! What has she ever got from this man but hard words and insults? Why, I have seen her start when he spoke to her, as though a gun had gone off. No, no; if first-love ever lasts for ever, man, it is only when one has had no experience of it. Not that I mean to say you will soon get tired of Lilian, you know; that's quite a different matter."

"Indeed, sir, I think that I shall not do that," answered Walter, blushing; for he could not but reflect who had been his first-love, and how it would astonish his future father-in-law to learn that it had not been Lilian, but that counterfeit presentment of her (as she had been), her sister. Ill-usage, and the destruction of her brightest illusions, had altered poor Lotty, indeed, since that memorable occasion when he had travelled in her company to Penaddon; but, for the moment, he seemed to see her as she had looked that day.

" Has Sir Reginald returned to London?" inquired Walter after a long pause, during which both he and his companion were deep in thought.

" No," replied Mr. Brown ; " or rather, he did return, but found the place too hot to hold him. The news of his conduct here had arrived before him. I hear from one of my correspondents that he was cut at his club, which it appears is the severest chastisement society can inflict, though I daresay he is too thick-skinned to feel it."

" You are wrong there, sir," answered Walter gravely ; " that is just what he would feel—the very punishment, of all others, under which his undoubted courage would not sustain him."

" Still it would have been more satisfactory to learn that he was hanged," observed the old merchant grimly ; " instead of which he has only been transported."

" Transported ! How do you mean?"

" Oh, I forgot I had not told you. He has gone to live in Paris, with—with"— it was Mr. Brown's turn to blush now, and

he did it in a very unmistakable manner—
" with that aunt of his, of whom we used to
see so much at Willowbank, Mrs. Sheldon.
There must be something good about that
woman to make her thus stick to him in his
disgrace, and give him what countenance
she can."

"Doubtless; yet I think she was a de-
signing woman."

"Very likely," answered Mr. Brown
drily; " widows often are."

Then there was another pause, even
longer than the preceding. " Walter, my
lad, observed the old merchant, as he threw
away the end of his cigar, "what on earth
was it made you come to Sicily ?"

" Well, sir," answered Walter, smiling, " I
was advised to do so." Of course there
would have been no harm now in confessing
the true reason for his exodus, but that
would have reopened the whole matter of
Reginald's ill-conduct—the suspicions that
Lilian had entertained of him, &c.—and
the topic had been already sufficiently
debated.

" Advised ? What! by a doctor, do you
mean ? Considering how fortunate the

issue has been for me, I think he deserves a fee."

" Well, no, sir ; it was not a doctor, but a very good friend—a painter. If it had not been for his suggestion, I certainly should not have had the opportunity of doing you the service which you are pleased to value at such a fancy price."

"Then that man's pictures shall never want a buyer," cried Mr. Brown excitedly. " What's his name and address ?"

" His name is Pelter, and he occupies lodgings in the same house with me in Beech Street. He is a very good artist, though by no means a very successful one ; his style——"

" I don't care what his style is," interrupted the merchant in his old arbitrary way, "for I mean to like it whatever it is. I shall buy what he can't sell, and give him orders for all he paints for the future. If he is your friend, my lad, he is my friend, and I shall make a point of patronizing him."

" Indeed, sir," answered Walter, smiling, " I hope you will not attempt to do that."

He had a letter from his friend in his

pocket at that very time, the second he had received from him—though Jack was as dilatory with his pen as with his brush—since the Corralli affair had been noised abroad; preaching Bohemianism and independence of all sorts, with a private and particular exception in favour of a man who had won an heiress, as a simple knight of old might carry off a king's daughter in a tournament, by his courage and conduct among brigands. "I was convinced, my dear Walter, from the first, that, sooner or later, you would swerve from the faith, and become a domestic character. You will have trouble in the flesh—not to mention the spirits—but I spare you. I believe nature intended you to be a married man in what is satirically termed 'easy circumstances;' nor should I be surprised to see you (afar off) glistening in the sun, even as those who wear polished boots in the daytime. It is the privilege of some, whose friends have been thus turned away from them, to become godfathers to their children, but I am afraid I am hardly fit for even that connexion. Still there will be a link between us, old friend, though it may not be publicly acknowledged. I am indebted to you for many an hour of 'sweet companionship,' the memory of which will always be a treasure to me; the old house here is desolate enough without you, and I dare not go into your rooms; yet it is well for me that I have known and loved you. But 'this is sentiment, sir,' as old Tintac says, when he has concluded his bargain, and can eulogize 'a picture of the affections,' as his own. Talking of pictures, .Nellie Neale has been here to break to me the news that she can no longer be a model, except of the domestic virtues. She is going to be married to a respectable young fellow in her own rank of life, with which prospect she bids me tell you she is quite content. This is to me a 'dark saying,' unless indeed she flatters herself that she might have had Walter Litton, Esq., for the asking. With that young gentleman, it seems it is always Leap-year. Your relations with the Self-made One are indeed a subject for congratulation, and must have afforded you enormous opportunities; surely, surely you have not neglected to take sketches of him when in captivity. Let me suggest a series—*Corralli after Brown: Brown before Corralli: Brown on the Mountain: a Storm: Brown in female Brigand Costume, escaping: Brown laid lifeless by (the wind of) a Musket-bullet.* Keep these by you in the rough; and if anything should disturb your present relations with him, threaten to touch them up—in which my assistance may be of some service, and *publish* them. *Verbum sap.*"

This was a letter, though very significant of the writer, which Walter could hardly show in its entirety to Mr. Brown, so he confined himself to a *vivâ voce* description of his friend's characteristics.

"I see," observed the old merchant good-humouredly; "this young gentleman is as proud and independent as his friend; he will have no patron but the dealers, wont he? Then the dealers shall buy them—for me."

The old merchant was as good as his word. It was most surprising—and to no one more than to Jack himself—how very much the demand for Mr. Pelter's pictures increased among the trade from the spring of that date; the effect of which did not much appear indeed in the attire or mode of life of that modest artist, but was very perceptible in the furniture of his studio; for, partly hidden, partly bulging forth under the folds of a picturesque Spanish cloak, hung low, for the purpose of concealing it, was always to be seen in that apartment a vast circular object bound with iron hoops. Jack took in his stout by the barrel.

His apprehensions of a separation from his friend, let us add, were altogether without foundation. Lilian was by no means one of those women who exhibit their devotion to the object of their choice by isolating him from all whom he held dear before his marriage; she made his friend her friend, and bound her Walter closer to herself, if that were possible, by that new tie. Jack was a frequent and welcome guest at Willowbank, and had at least one prejudice in common with its proprietor: they stood shoulder to shoulder against the practice of putting on evening attire, except on very great occasions. At dinner-parties in the dog-days Mr. Brown was compelled to wear black broad-cloth, whereas Jack sent his excuses, and sat at home in his

shirt-sleeves, with his kind heart full of
pity for the victims of society.   He had the
run of the house, except one Bluebeard's
chamber, in which were hung his own pictures, until one day a great City magnate,
who knew what was good when he saw it,
even out of a soup-tureen, offered to buy the
whole lot for twice the fancy price that his
host had given for them.   Mr. Brown hesitated as to whether he should sell, and send
the difference by cheque to Jack—which
would probably have cost him his friendship.   As it was he adopted another plan.
The next time Jack came he was shown into
that very room, and just as his brow was
getting black with pride and shame (for he
guessed all in a moment)—" No wonder you
are rather moved, Mr. Pelter," said the old
gentleman, " for I could make fifteen hundred pounds by those pictures to-morrow.
However, old Ingot has taken a fancy to
your works, and I reckon I shall never get
another bargain out of you again."   A
remark which had not only delicacy but
truth to recommend it, for there is now
many a R.A. whose signature on canvas
counts far less than that of plain Jack

Pelter. "It is as good as my name on stamped paper," boasts Mr. Christopher Brown, "or as our Walter's Word."

But we are sadly anticipating matters. These things occurred of course long after the two chief personages in the history had been made one.

In the early spring-time, when the flowers were thick upon the grave of Joanna, which was in the very spot which he whom she loved had at one time thought himself to rest, Walter and Lilian were married. It was a very quiet wedding, and yet it was a double one, for Francisco and Julia were united on the same day; nor did the merchant forget the share which the young Sicilian had had in effecting his release from captivity, or that his bride had been Lilian's tender and faithful nurse for many a weary week. Her place as attendant upon Mrs. Walter Litton was supplied by a handsome young woman, wearing the garb of woe, which, however, became her admirably, and who was not so prostrated by the loss of one swain but that she had already given hopes to several others that they might occupy his shoes. A more charming *sou-*

brette, in fact, than Lavocca was transformed into—nor a more modest one withal, in spite of her little flirtations—it would have been difficult to find. She left, however, all native lovers despairing, and stepped on board the *Sylphide* fancy-free. The whole party went straight to England in the yacht, their original idea of visiting Rome being abandoned. In vain the banker and other English friends painted the beauties of Italian scenery, and the interest of classical antiquities, in the most attractive colours, as also the safety of the highways and railroads. There were brigands in Italy as well as in Sicily, and Mr. Brown was resolved to run no risks. The state of Lilian's health had alone detained him thus long upon foreign soil, and he was heartily glad to quit it. He had lost, not indeed fifty thousand pounds, he was wont to say, but still a good many pounds—of flesh—while partaking of the hospitality of Captain Corralli, and his health needed to be recruited at home.

Let us take a last look of our friends as they stand upon the deck of the *Sylphide*, and wave their hands in farewell to those

upon the quay. The consul is there, who
strove so gallantly, although in vain, to
assist poor Walter in his strait, and who
has long got to know and like the young
fellow; the banker also, at whose hospitable
table—though he little thought to have
been able to accept an invitation from him
—Walter has often dined, and talked over
with him that matter of the " Brown
Ransom," which is to this day the stock
story of the house of Gordon. Francisco is
there with his new-made bride, and kisses
his brown hand in graceful good-bye, while
she sheds silent tears. Signor Baccari is
also in tears, by no means silent ones, but
his grief at the departure of his lodger is no
less genuine than demonstrative. Again
and again he commends Walter to the
protection of the saints, and bids him
beware of brigands—a baleful product,
which he fancies to be indigenous to every
soil. The yacht is loosened from her
moorings, sail after sail clothes her delicate
spars, and off she glides towards England.
The figures of those upon the quay grow
fainter and fainter, till only the fluttering
kerchief can be made out which marks Julia's

presence ; but the noble hills which are being left for ever are still discernible. To one of these, that stands up straight and sheer to eastward, Walter points in silence, and presses Lilian's arm.

"Yes; that was once my prison," she answers, for in it was Joanna's cavern. "I do not, however, regret my captivity, since but for it you would not have been mine, Walter."

Here she pauses, gazing up into his face with inexpressible love; then, as if remorseful for forgetting the woes of others in her own exceeding happiness, her eyes wander to Lotty—husbandless—deprived of what she has gained. "She is happier thus, than she could ever have been with *him*," whispered Walter, in answer to her thought. And indeed, as she stood smiling cheerfully, with her hand upon her father's arm, and in loving converse with him, it might well be hoped that that well-nigh broken heart would heal.

THE END.